"Your sister ... marry..."

Bethany's face gre[...] [...]y grow on trees in New Covenant."

"Anyone you chose would be getting a fine wife."

She looked up to study Michael's reflection in the glass, but it wasn't clear enough to let her see what he was thinking. "Are you making me an offer?"

"You would be getting a very poor bargain if I was."

She turned around so she could look into his eyes. "Why do you say that?"

"Because it's the truth."

There was so much pain in his voice and deep in his eyes that she wanted to hold him and promise to make everything better.

She couldn't. "What's wrong, Michael?"

"Nothing that you can fix."

"How do I know that if you can't tell me what troubles you?"

"Trust me. You don't want to know." He turned and walked down the hall and out the back door.

He was so wrong.

Bethany wanted to know everything about Michael Shetler.

After thirty-five years as a nurse, **Patricia Davids** hung up her stethoscope to become a full-time writer. She enjoys spending her free time visiting her grandchildren, doing some long-overdue yard work and traveling to research her story locations. She resides in Wichita, Kansas. Patricia always enjoys hearing from her readers. You can visit her online at patriciadavids.com.

Books by Patricia Davids

Love Inspired

North Country Amish

An Amish Wife for Christmas

The Amish Bachelors

An Amish Harvest
An Amish Noel
His Amish Teacher
Their Pretend Amish Courtship
Amish Christmas Twins
An Unexpected Amish Romance
His New Amish Family

Brides of Amish Country

Plain Admirer
Amish Christmas Joy
The Shepherd's Bride
The Amish Nanny
An Amish Family Christmas: A Plain Holiday
An Amish Christmas Journey
Amish Redemption

Visit the Author Profile page at Harlequin.com for more titles.

An Amish Wife
for Christmas

Patricia Davids

 LOVE INSPIRED BOOKS

Recycling programs
for this product may
not exist in your area.

ISBN-13: 978-1-335-42840-0

An Amish Wife for Christmas

Copyright © 2018 by Patricia MacDonald

www.Harlequin.com

Printed in U.S.A.

That he would grant you, according to the riches of his glory, to be strengthened with might by his Spirit in the inner man; That Christ may dwell in your hearts by faith; that ye, being rooted and grounded in love, May be able to comprehend with all saints what is the breadth, and length, and depth, and height; And to know the love of Christ, which passeth knowledge, that ye might be filled with all the fullness of God.

—*Ephesians* 3:16–19

This book is dedicated with great admiration to my longtime and dare I say long-suffering editor, Emily Rodmell. I'm sure I have tried your endless patience far more often than any other author, but you have never failed to help me get back on track. During the bleak moments of my personal life and in some weird and crazy times you have remained confident in my talent and pushed me to write a better book even when I wasn't sure I wanted to go there. Thanks for your faith in me. Here's hoping it isn't misplaced. Onward and upward.

Chapter One

"Your brother's behavior reflects badly on you, Bethany, and on our community. Something must be done."

Bethany Martin sat across from Bishop Elmer Schultz at her kitchen table with her head bowed and her hands clasped tightly together in her lap. Her dear friend Gemma Lapp sat beside her. Bethany was grateful for Gemma's moral support.

"We Amish are newcomers here," he continued. "We can't afford to stir ill will among our *Englisch* neighbors. Don't you agree?"

Bethany glanced up and met his intense gaze. She nodded slightly. An imposing man in his mid-fifties, the bishop had a shaggy gray-and-black beard that reached to the middle of his chest. A potato farmer and owner of a shed building business, he was known for his long and often rambling sermons, but he was a fair man and well liked in their small Amish community. Bethany didn't take his visit lightly. She prepared to defend her brother.

"Ivan isn't a bad boy. It's just that he misses his grandfather. He's angry that God took Elijah from us and he feels guilty. The two of them were very close." Her heart ached for her troubled brother.

"Time will heal this," Gemma added.

The bishop sighed. "Your grandfather Elijah was a fine man, Bethany. I have no doubt that he kept the boy's high spirits in check, but Ivan has quickly put one foot on the slippery slope that leads to serious trouble. He needs a firm hand to guide him and mold him into an upstanding and righteous man."

"I can do that," Bethany assured him. "I've raised Ivan from the time he was five and our sister, Jenny, wasn't much more than a newborn babe." She might be their sister, but she was also the only mother they had ever known. Both mother and father to them after the man who bore that title left his family for the fourth and final time. Bethany's anger surged to the surface but she quickly brought it under control. At least her mother had been spared knowing about his final betrayal. She had been positive he would return to care for his children after she was gone. He hadn't. Bethany brought her attention back to the matter at hand.

Gemma waved one hand. "Ivan is almost fourteen. Boys that age get into mischief."

It was a weak argument and Bethany knew it. Her brother's recent behavior was more than mischief, but she didn't know what to do about it. He seemed to be done listening to her.

The bishop's expression softened. "Bethany, your grandfather was concerned that you have sacrificed your chance to have a family of your own in order to care for your siblings."

She drew herself up straight. "I don't feel that way. Ivan and Jenny *are* my family."

The bishop laced his fingers together on the table. "I am the spiritual leader of this community and as such I have a duty to oversee the welfare of all my flock. Normally I would leave the discipline of children to their parents. In this case I feel duty bound to step in. Elijah was my dear friend. It was his vision that founded our new community here. It was his desire to see it grow. For that we need the goodwill of our *Englisch* neighbors."

"I'm aware of that. I spent many months helping him search for the best place to settle. New Covenant is as much my dream as it was his." She didn't like the direction the bishop seemed to be going.

"Then you agree that we can't let the reckless actions of one boy ruin what has been created."

"He isn't trying to spoil anything." Bethany was compelled to defend Ivan, but the truth was she didn't know what was wrong with him. Was he acting out because of his grief or was something else going on?

His schoolwork had suffered in the past weeks. His teacher had complained of behavior issues in class. He had been in several scuffles with non-Amish boys earlier in the year but they weren't anything serious. It was his recent secrecy and withdrawal that bothered Bethany the most. How could she help him if she didn't understand what was amiss?

She lifted her chin. "There is no proof that he damaged Greg Janson's tractor or that he is responsible for letting Robert Morris's cattle loose."

Bishop Schultz leveled a stern look at her. "He was seen near both farms at the time and he'd been in fights with both the Janson and Morris boys."

"That's not proof," she insisted.

The bishop pushed back from the table. "I have written to your uncle in Bird-in-Hand."

She frowned. "To Onkel Harvey? Why?"

"Elijah mentioned that Harvey and his family plan to visit you this Christmas."

"That's true. We are expecting them to stay a week as they were unable to come to the funeral."

The bishop rose to his feet. "I have asked your uncle to take Ivan with him when the family returns to Pennsylvania."

Bethany's mouth dropped open. "*Nee*, you can't send Ivan away. This isn't right."

"It was not an easy decision. I know your intentions are *goot* but the boy needs the firm guidance of a man. You are too easy on him."

"Because he's still a little boy." The situation was quickly slipping out of her control. They couldn't take her brother from her. Fear sent her pulse pounding in her temples. "Please, Bishop, you must reconsider."

"I will not."

Bethany pressed both hands to her heart. "I promised my mother before she died that I would keep the family together. I promised her. Don't do this."

The bishop's expression didn't change. Her plea had fallen on deaf ears. Men were the decision makers in her Amish community. The bishop had the last word even in this family matter.

He took his coat and hat from the pegs by the door and put them on. "Bethany, if you were married I wouldn't have to take this course of action. Your husband would be the one to make such decisions and discipline the boy. With Elijah gone,

I see no other choice. I must think of what is best for all, not just for one."

He nodded to her and left. Bethany wanted to cry, to shout at him, to run after him and beg him to change his mind, but she knew it wouldn't do any good.

"I'm sorry." Gemma laid a hand on Bethany's shoulder.

"What am I going to do? There has to be a way to change the bishop's mind."

"Why don't I make us some toast and a cup of coffee. Then we'll put our heads together and come up with a plan."

"We're out of bread and I don't want any coffee."

"What Amish woman runs out of bread?"

"This one. There has been so much to do since Daadi's passing I haven't had time to bake. If Ivan straightens up and starts behaving, if he apologizes to the bishop maybe he'll be allowed to stay. It's five weeks until Christmas. That's enough time to prove he has changed."

"Or you can get married. That will fix everything."

Bethany gave her friend an exasperated look. Gemma knew Bethany's feeling about marriage. It wasn't for her. "It's unlikely that I could find someone to wed me before Christmas, Gemma."

"If you weren't so particular, maybe not. Jesse Crump holds you in high regard."

Bethany wrinkled her nose. "Having a conversation with Jesse is like pulling teeth. He's a nice enough fellow, but he never has anything to say."

"Ack, you're too fussy by far."

"You marry him."

Both Gemma's eyebrows shot up. "Me? Not a chance. Besides, it isn't my brother that is being sent away."

Bethany battled her rising panic. "I wish Daadi were still here. I don't know what to do."

Gemma slipped an arm around Bethany's shoulders and gave her a hug. "If your grandfather was still alive we wouldn't be having this conversation."

"I know."

Ivan's troubling behavior had started when their grandfather became ill early in the fall but it had gotten much worse since his death. Her gaze moved to the closed door leading to her grandfather's workroom. Their grandfather had happily spent hours repairing clocks and antique watches during the long winter months in his tiny shop. With the door open she used to hear him humming or muttering depending on how a particular project was progressing.

The workshop hadn't been opened since Ivan found Elijah slumped over his desk barely breathing. The boy ran to find help but by the time it arrived Elijah was gone.

She should have mailed his unfinished works back to their owners before now but she couldn't bear to enter the room. The grief she tried so hard to control would come pouring out when she did.

Tears stung the backs of her eyelids, but she quickly blinked them away. The quiet strength and unquestioning love of her grandfather had seen Bethany through the worst times in her life. It was still hard to accept that she could never turn to him for guidance again.

She drew a deep breath and squared her shoulders. He would tell her prayer and hard work solved problems. Worry and regret never did. There had to be a way to keep her family together and she would find it. Perhaps her uncle would side with her. She would write her own letter to him and plead her case.

She slipped into her coat. "Thank you for coming today, Gemma, but I'd best get the rest of my chores done."

Gemma followed her to the door. "I don't know how you'll manage this farm without Elijah and Ivan."

"One day at a time and with the help of our neighbors if I need it."

"I've never known you to ask for help." Gemma moved to put on her black bonnet and coat.

"I asked you to sit with me when the bishop came today, didn't I?"

Gemma rolled her eyes. "Okay, you have asked for help one time. I wish I knew what to say but I think it is all up to Ivan. I'm surprised he wasn't here this morning."

"He's at school. I didn't want to take him out of class."

The New Covenant Amish community was too small yet to have their own school. The five Amish children in their church, including her brother and sister, attended the nearest public school. It was far from ideal but the teachers and school board had taken great pains to accommodate the needs and customs of the new Amish pupils.

The two women walked outside together. Gemma pulled on her gloves. "Do you want me to come over this evening when you talk to him?"

Bethany shook her head. "*Danki*, but I think it's best I speak to him alone."

"All right. I'll stop by tomorrow and you can tell me all about it." The two women exchanged a hug. Gemma climbed into her buggy and drove away.

Bethany's breath rose as puffs of white mist in the chilly mid-November morning as she crossed the snow-covered yard to the newly completed red barn. It was the latest building to be added to the new community. The bulk of the structure had been raised in a single day with the help of an Amish community from upstate New York. Thirty men had traveled all night by bus and worked feverishly to complete the barn before taking the long bus ride home again that night. Someday the people of New Covenant would return the favor.

Her grandfather had had plans for half a dozen additional structures to attract more Amish families to New Covenant. It had been his dream to form a thriving Amish district in Maine, far from the tourist centers in Pennsylvania. To him, fewer tourists meant less money but more time to spend close to God and family without worldly influences. If only he could have lived to see his dream grow and thrive.

Bethany fed and watered the chickens, gathered the eggs and then fed and watered the geese before heading to the barn. Her mind wasn't on her chores. Her conversation with the bishop replayed in her head as she fed and watered their two horses. Outside the milk cow's stall, Bethany paused and leaned on her pitchfork. "I've got trouble, Clarabelle."

The cow didn't answer her. Bethany pitched a forkful of hay to the family's placid brown-and-white Guernsey and then leaned on the stall door. "The bishop has decided to send Ivan to Bird-in-

Hand to live with Onkel Harvey. It's not right. It's not fair. I can't bear the idea of sending my little brother away. It will break his heart and Jenny's, to say nothing of mine. We belong together."

Clarabelle munched a mouthful of hay as she regarded Bethany with soulful deep brown eyes. The bell around her neck clanked softly as she tilted her head to allow Bethany to scratch behind her left ear. Bethany complied. As a confidant, Clarabelle was unassuming and easy to talk to, but she was short on advice.

"Advice is what I need, Clarabelle. The bishop said Ivan could stay if I had a husband. Someone to discipline and guide the boy. I don't believe for a minute that is the solution but I'm getting desperate. Any idea where I can get a husband before Christmas? And please don't suggest Jesse Crump. Jedidiah Zook might be a possibility if he smiled more. Maybe he just needs a wife to make him happier. What do you think?"

"I doubt your cow has the answers you seek but if she does I have a few questions for her about my own problems," a man said in an amused drawl.

Bethany spun around. A stranger stood in the open barn door. He wore a black Amish hat pulled low on his forehead and a dark blue woolen coat with the collar turned up against the cold.

He carried a duffel bag over one shoulder and he leaned on a black cane.

The mirth sparkling in his eyes sent a flush of heat to her cheeks. How humiliating. To be caught talking to a cow about matrimonial prospects made her look ridiculous.

She struggled to hide her embarrassment. After looking the man up and down, she stabbed the pitchfork into the hay again and dumped it into Clarabelle's stall. "It's rude to eavesdrop on a private conversation."

"I'm not sure talking to a cow qualifies as a private conversation but I am sorry to intrude." The man put down his duffel bag.

He didn't look sorry. He looked like he was struggling not to laugh at her. At least he was a stranger. Maybe this mortifying episode wouldn't become known in the community. She cringed at the thought of Jedidiah Zook hearing the story. "How can I help you?"

"Mind if I sit here for a minute?" He pointed to a stack of straw bales beside the barn door.

She wanted him to go away but her Amish upbringing prevented her from suggesting it. Any stranger in need deserved her help.

He didn't wait for her reply but limped to the closest bale and sat down with a weary sigh. "The bus driver who dropped me off said New Covenant was a little way along on this road. His idea of a little way does not match mine."

"It's less than half a mile to the highway from my lane."

He rubbed his leg. "That's the farthest I've walked in six months. How much farther do I have to go?"

"You have arrived at the south end of our community."

He tipped his head slightly. "I thought New Covenant was a town."

"It's more a collection of houses strung out on either side of the road right now, but it will be a thriving village one day." She prayed she spoke the truth.

"Glad to hear it. I'm Michael Shetler, by the way." He took off his hat and raked his fingers through his thick dark brown hair.

She considered not giving him her name. The less he knew to repeat the better.

He noticed her hesitation and cleared his throat. "It's rude not to introduce yourself in return."

She arched one eyebrow. "I'm being rude? That's the pot calling the kettle black. I am Bethany Martin," she admitted, hoping she wasn't making a mistake.

"Nice to meet you, Bethany. Once I've had a rest I'll step outside if you want to finish your private conversation." He winked. One corner of his mouth twitched, revealing a dimple in his cheek.

Something about the sparkle in his blue eyes invited her to smile back at him but she firmly resisted the urge. She stabbed the pitchfork into the remaining hay and left it standing upright. "I'm glad I could supply you with some amusement today."

"It's been a long time since I've had something to smile about."

The clatter of hooves outside caught her attention as a horse and wagon pulled up beside the barn and stopped. She caught a glimpse of the driver through the open door. He stood and faced the barn. "Ivan Martin, are you in there? It's Jedidiah Zook. I want to speak to you!"

Her gaze shot to Michael. His grin widened. Her heart sank as he chuckled. "I may not have given Clarabelle enough credit. It seems your preferred beau has arrived. It was Jedidiah Zook you hoped would come courting, right?"

She glared and shook a finger at him. "Don't you dare repeat one word of what you heard in here."

Michael couldn't help teasing her. The high color in her cheeks and the fire in her eyes told him she was no meek Amish maid. He wagged his eyebrows. "Do you need a go-between? Shall

I speak on your behalf? I'll be happy to help any way I can."

"If you say anything, I'll… I'll…" She clamped her lips closed. The sheen of unshed tears gathered in her eyes, but she quickly blinked them back and raised her chin.

Teasing was one thing. Upsetting her was another. He held up one hand. "Relax. Your secret is safe with me. If the cow spills the beans, that is not my fault."

"Stay here." Bethany rushed past him out the wide double doors. "*Guder mariye*, Jedidiah. Ivan isn't in here. He's at school. Can I be of any help?"

"Your brother has gone too far this time."

The man's angry voice brought Michael closer to the open door to watch. Bethany faced Jedidiah defiantly with her head up and her hands on her hips. "What has he done?"

"Two thirty-pound bags of potatoes and a ten-pound bag of dried beans are missing from my cellar."

"What makes you think Ivan took them?"

"Because he sold a bag of potatoes to the general store owner just this morning."

She folded her arms in front of her. "That's not proof he took them. Maybe it was one of our sacks that he sold."

"Was it?"

"I'm not sure."

"You tell him I came by and that I'm on my way to report this theft to the bishop. This has gone beyond what can be ignored. It must stop. If you can't control the boy someone else will have to." He lifted the reins, turned the wagon around and headed down the lane.

Michael limped out to stand beside her. "Not a very jolly fellow. Are you sure he's the one?"

She shot him a sour look. "In spite of what you think you heard earlier, I am not in the market for a husband."

Why wasn't she married already? She was certainly attractive enough. Not that he was in the market for a relationship. He wasn't. He might never be. He sobered at the thought. The men who shot him and robbed the store he had worked may have robbed him of a family, too. He had no idea if his PTSD would get better living in the isolation of northern Maine, but it was his last option.

Bethany brushed past him into the barn, a fierce scowl marring her pretty features. "I need to speak to my brother and get to the bottom of this. You are welcome to rest here."

He was glad he wasn't the brother in question. She went down the aisle and opened the stall door of a black mare with a white blaze. She led the mare out, tied the horse to a hitching post and began to harness her.

"Let me do that for you." He took a step closer.

"I can manage," she snapped.

He took a step back and held one hand up. She didn't need or want his help. In short order she had the harness on and then led the animal outside, where she backed the mare in between the shafts of the buggy parked in a lean-to at the side of the building.

"May I?" he asked, pointing to the buggy. She nodded. He finished securing the traces on one side while she did the other. He buckled the crupper, the loop that went around the mare's tail to keep the harness from sliding forward on the animal, as Bethany finished her side and came to check his work.

"Danki."

She thanked him like it was a chore. Bethany Martin was clearly used to doing things by herself.

Michael realized that he hadn't looked over his shoulder once since hearing Bethany's voice. That had to be some kind of record. He glanced around out of habit but there was nothing sinister in the farmstead and empty snow-covered fields that backed up to wooded hills on either side of the wide valley. All throughout his trip to New Covenant he'd been on edge, expecting danger from every stranger that came close to him. He'd spent most of the bus ride from Philadelphia with sweating palms and tense muscles, expecting another attack or a flashback to overtake him at any second. They never came when he was expecting them.

He rubbed a hand across the back of his neck. For the first time in weeks the knots in his neck and shoulders were missing. Maybe he was getting better. Maybe this move was the right thing, after all. He prayed it was. Nothing here reminded him of the Philadelphia street or the shop where his life had changed so drastically.

Here the air was fresh and clean. The next house was several hundred yards up the road. Nothing crowded him. He could start over here. No one would look at him with pity or worse. He had a job waiting for him in New Covenant and a place to live all thanks to the generosity of a man he'd never met. He needed to get going, but he was reluctant to leave Bethany's company for some reason. Her no-nonsense attitude was comforting. He pushed the thought aside. "I should be on my way. Can you give me directions to Elijah Troyer's farm?"

She shot him a startled look and then glanced away. "This was his farm," she said softly with a quiver in her voice.

"Was? He sold it?" Michael waited impatiently for her to speak.

She kept her gaze averted. "I'm sorry but Elijah Troyer passed away three weeks ago."

Michael drew back with a sharp intake of breath. "He's dead? That can't be."

He fought against the onrush of panic. What about the job? What about the place to live? Were his hopes for a new life dead, too?

Chapter Two

Bethany watched as Michael limped away and sat down on the hay bale inside the barn door. He rubbed his face with both hands. She could see he was deeply affected by the news of her grandfather's death. Sympathy made her soften her tone. "I'm sorry to give you the sad news. Did you know my grandfather well?"

Michael shook his head. "I never met him."

If he didn't know her grandfather, why was he so shaken by his passing? As much as she wanted to stay and find out Michael's connection to Elijah, she had to speak to Ivan as soon as possible. If he had stolen the potatoes and beans as Jedidiah claimed, the items would have to be returned at once, but there had to be some mistake. Her brother wasn't a thief.

Please let it be a mistake, Lord.

The bishop would never reconsider sending

Ivan to live with Onkel Harvey if Jedidiah's claim was true.

She slipped the reins through the slot under the winter windshield of the buggy. "I'm sorry you didn't have a chance to meet my grandfather. He was a wonderful man."

"He offered me a job working for him. Is that job still available?"

"I know nothing about such an offer. Are you sure it was my grandfather who promised you work?"

"Elijah Troyer, in New Covenant, Maine. That's what the letter said. Is there another Elijah Troyer in the community?"

"There is not. I don't know what my grandfather had in mind, but I can't afford to hire someone right now."

"I was also told I would have a place to stay. I reckon if there's no job there's no lodging, either?"

Was he talking about the small cabin that sat at the back of her property? Her grandfather had mentioned readying it for a tenant before he became ill, but she didn't know if he had finished the repairs. Besides, she wasn't ready to host a lodger. Nor did she want to leave Michael Shetler like this. He appeared dazed and lost. Her heart went out to him.

"You should speak to our bishop, Elmer Schultz. I'm sure he can help. He won't be at home this time of day, but I can give you a ride to his place of business."

"It seems I don't have much choice. *Danki.*"

Michael slowly climbed into the passenger seat. Bethany walked around the back and got in on the driver's side. She picked up the reins. "The school is about three miles from here."

"I thought we were going to the bishop's place of business."

"We are but I must stop at the school first. I hope you don't mind."

"As long as I don't have to walk three miles I don't mind."

From the corner of her eye Bethany noticed him rubbing his leg frequently. It must pain him a great deal. This close to him she noticed the dark circles under his eyes, as if he hadn't slept well. He was pale, too. She sat silent for the first half mile of their trip but her curiosity about Michael got the better of her. "Where are you from?"

"My family lives in Holmes County, Ohio. My father and brother have a construction business in Sugarcreek."

"Did you work in construction with them?"

"Nee." He didn't elaborate.

"I've heard that's a large Amish community. Do you have a lot of tourists who visit there?"

"We do."

"Like where I am from. Bird-in-Hand, Pennsylvania. My grandfather wanted to start a community that wasn't dependent on tourism. Don't get me wrong, he knew how important the industry is to many Amish who can't make a living farming, but it wasn't the lifestyle he wanted to live."

Michael pulled his coat tighter. "There had to be warmer places to settle."

She chuckled as she looked out over the snow-covered fields that flanked the road. "The coldest part of the winter has yet to come."

"So why here?"

"The price of land and the ability to purchase farms large enough to support big families were more of a consideration than the weather. Plus, we were warmly welcomed by the people here. Many local families have been here for generations. They like the idea that we want to be here and farm for generations, too. A lot of the elders in the community remember farming with horses when they were children. Folks are very independent minded in Maine. They know what hard work is. When someone has to sell farmland they would rather sell it to the Amish because we will live on it and farm it as their grandparents did. They consider it preferable to selling to a large farming corporation intent on grabbing up as much land as possible."

"What do you grow here besides snowdrifts?"

She smiled. "Potatoes. Maine is the third-largest producer of potatoes in the United States. Broccoli grows well in the cool climate as do many other vegetables."

"As long as you don't get an early freeze."

"That's true of farming in Ohio or almost anywhere."

"I guess you're right about that."

The main highway followed the curve of the river and after another mile Fort Craig came into view. Bethany turned off the highway into a residential area at the outskirts of town. The elementary school was located in a cul-de-sac at the end of the street.

As she drew the horse to a stop in front of the school she noticed several of the classes were out at recess. She stepped down from the buggy and caught sight of her sister, Jenny, playing with several other girls on the swings. Jenny spotted her and ran over. "Sister, what are you doing here?"

"I've come to speak to Ivan. Did he get on the bus with you this morning?"

Jenny shook her head. "*Nee*, he said Jeffrey's mom was going to bring him to school."

"And did she?"

"I don't know. Sister, I have *wunderbar goot* news."

Bethany crouched to meet Jenny's gaze. "Have you seen Ivan today?"

Jenny screwed up her face as she concentrated. "I don't think so. You should ask his teacher."

Bethany stood upright. "That's exactly what I plan to do."

"Don't you want to hear my news?"

"In a minute."

Jenny's happy expression faded. Michael got out of the buggy. He took several stiff steps. "I just need to stretch my legs a little."

"Who is that?" Jenny asked in a loud whisper.

Bethany was inpatient to find Ivan but she made the introduction. "This is Michael Shetler. He's a newcomer. This is my sister, Jenny."

He nodded toward her. "I'm pleased to meet you, Jenny. I'd love to hear your news."

"You would?" Jenny asked hopefully.

"Sure. It must be important. You look ready to burst."

Jenny smiled from ear to ear. "I got picked to be in the community Christmas play. I'm going to be the aerator."

Bethany looked at Michael. He returned her questioning gaze and shook his head slightly. Jenny was bouncing up and down with happiness.

Bethany smiled at her. "That is *wunderbar*. What does the aerator do?"

"I get to tell everyone the Christmas story in English and in Pennsylvania Dutch while the other kids act out the scenes. Ivan is going to sing a song by himself."

From the corner of her eye, Bethany saw Michael rub a hand across his mouth to hide a grin. Bethany was afraid she'd start laughing if she looked at him again. Learning English as a second language was difficult for many Amish children who spoke only Pennsylvania Dutch until they started school. "I'm sure you will make a *goot* narrator if you practice hard."

"I'll practice lots and lots if you help me."

"You know I will."

"I need to have an angel costume, too. I'm going to be an angel aerator."

"Angel *narrator*," Michael corrected her in a gentle tone.

"Narrator," Jenny replied slowly. He nodded and she grinned at him.

Bethany patted her sister's head. "We'll talk about it when you come home from school this evening."

"Okay." Jenny took off to rejoin her friends.

"Cute kid," Michael said, still grinning. "How many siblings do you have?"

"Just Jenny and Ivan. Excuse me while I check on him." Bethany headed through the front doors of the school. She found the eighth-grade room and looked in through the open door. Ivan wasn't in his seat. His best friend, Jeffrey, was missing, too.

A bell sounded in the empty hall, startling her. The boys and girls in the room filed to the back to gather their coats, mittens and hats from hooks before rushing past her to get outside. After the last child exited the room Bethany stepped inside. "Ms. Kenworthy, may I have a word with you?"

The teacher looked up from her desk. "Miss Martin, of course. Do come in. I was just getting ready to write a note to you."

"About Ivan?"

"Yes. I hope he is feeling better. He's missed almost an entire week of school. I have a list of homework assignments for him to complete and hand in when he returns."

Bethany's heart sank. "My brother is not sick at home."

"I see." Ms. Kenworthy opened a desk drawer and pulled out a sheet of notebook paper. "Then I assume you did not write this note?"

Bethany removed her gloves, took the note and quickly scanned it. It informed Ms. Kenworthy that Ivan would be out of school for a week due to his illness. It was signed with her name. Bethany sighed heavily and handed the letter back. "I did not write this. It is not my signature."

Ms. Kenworthy took the letter and replaced it in the drawer. "I thought it was odd that Jeffrey was the one who delivered it to me and not your sister. Do you know what Ivan has been doing instead of coming to school?"

"I wish I did. He doesn't confide in me these days."

"He was close to his grandfather, wasn't he?"

The understanding in the teacher's eyes allowed Bethany to unburden herself. "They were very close. Since Elijah's death Ivan has refused to talk to me about what's troubling him. He's changed so much. I was hoping he might have confided in you."

"I am deeply sorry for your loss. Elijah was well liked in this community."

"Thank you."

"Your brother's grades were not the best before your grandfather passed away. Since that time, he has earned nothing but Fs for incomplete work. Even when he is here he seems withdrawn until someone speaks to him. Then he's ready to start a fight over nothing. Unless he does extra-credit work and turns in his missing assignments, I'm afraid he is going to flunk the semester. I know that according to your religion this is his last year of education, but I still have to follow state guidelines. That puts me between a rock and a hard place. If he flunks the semester, he'll have to attend summer school."

Bethany shook her head. "Ivan will be needed

on the farm this summer. I don't see how we could spare him even a few hours a day."

"In that case he will have to repeat this grade next year. Talk to him. Try to make him see what's at stake." She removed a folder from another drawer. "Give these assignments to him. Hopefully he can finish most of them over the weekend."

"I will. Thank you." Bethany was angry with Ivan for his deceit, but she was more disappointed in herself. Where had she gone wrong? How had she failed him? She tried to be a parent to her siblings but without her grandfather's help she didn't know how to reach Ivan. Maybe letting him return to Pennsylvania would be for the best.

Except that it didn't feel like the right solution. She loved her brother. She couldn't imagine life without his annoying habits, constant teasing and his hearty laugh. She had to make him see that his actions were tearing the family apart.

But she needed to find him first. Clearly Jeffrey was in on whatever Ivan was up to. His parents lived a mile farther up into the woods from her home.

Bethany left the school building and saw Michael sitting on the buggy step. She'd forgotten him. A thin yellow hound lay a few feet away from him. The dog wagged its tail tentatively as it watched him. Michael pulled his gloves off and took something from his pocket. He held it toward the dog. The animal crept a few inches closer.

"Good girl," Michael said, tossing the item at the dog's feet. She snapped it up. At the sound of Bethany approaching, the dog darted for cover between two nearby parked cars.

Bethany stopped beside Michael. The dog grew bold enough to peek out from between the cars but didn't approach. "I see you made a new friend."

He rose to his feet. "She was sniffing at the trash cans and trying to get them open. I could see she was looking for a meal. I had a little left-over jerky I picked up on the bus ride here. She appears to need it more than I do. Is your brother at school?"

"*Nee*, but that doesn't prove he stole provisions from Jedidiah."

"You're still giving him the benefit of the doubt?"

"Of course. He's my brother."

"I hope your confidence isn't misplaced."

"I pray it's not but I will admit I'm at my wit's end. His teacher says he hasn't been to school all week. His friend gave the teacher a note that was signed with my name that said he was sick at home. I have to find out what's going on. He's left each morning to catch the school bus with his sister and he's walked home with her each evening, yet he hasn't been in school."

"Don't think too badly of him. Boys his age are sometimes impatient to grow up and live their own adventures. Then they make foolish mistakes because they aren't as smart as they think they are."

"Are you speaking from experience?"

"I am. My own."

"How many forged notes did you send to your teacher?"

A wry grin curved his lips. "My teacher happened to be my mother's youngest sister, so none."

"I'm afraid of what the bishop will say when Jedidiah tells his side of the story."

"If the bishop is a reasonable man he'll listen to your side of the story, as well."

She was grateful for his reassurance, but he didn't know how serious the situation was becoming. She held on to the hope that her uncle could be persuaded to let Ivan remain with her. "I will take you to see the bishop now."

"I appreciate that." He moved to open the buggy door for her and took her hand to help her in.

His grip was firm but his hand was soft. His skin lacked the calloused roughness of a man who made his living farming the land or woodworking. It wasn't the hand of a laborer, yet she found his gentle strength oddly comforting.

Perhaps he was a shopkeeper. Her grandfather had had plans to open a small grocery in New Covenant. Maybe that was the job he had promised Michael. It didn't matter. Her grandfather was gone, and she wasn't in a position to continue his work. At least not yet.

She looked up and met Michael's gaze as he continued to hold her hand longer than necessary. There was a profound sadness in the depth of his eyes that she didn't understand. What troubled him? What was he thinking?

Michael stared into Bethany's light blue eyes as the warmth of her touch went all the way to the center of his chest and warmed a place that had been cold for a long time. He studied her face, trying to find out why she triggered such a strong reaction in him.

Her pale blond hair was parted in the middle and worn under a white prayer covering. Her skin was fair with a scattering of freckles across her dainty nose. She was an attractive woman, too attractive for his peace of mind.

He let go of her hand, stepped away and limped around the back of the buggy, letting the pain in his leg remind him of why he had no business thinking about how perfectly her small hand had nestled in his. If things had been different, if he wasn't so damaged he would have enjoyed getting to know her better, but things weren't different. He had to accept that.

He also had more serious things to think about. He needed a job and he needed somewhere to live. Preferably a good distance away from other people in this remote community. His neighbors wouldn't appreciate being awakened in the middle of the night by the screams that sometimes accompanied his nightmares.

Thoughts of his dreams filled him with apprehension as his pulse shot up. He quickly scanned his surroundings. A car drove past the school, the tires crunching on the snow. Children were playing on the playground. He could hear their laughter and shouting. Someone stood at the corner of the school building. He thought it was a woman but he couldn't be sure. The person was bundled in a parka with the hood up. Perhaps a teacher watching the children. He struggled to convince himself that there was nothing sinister here but he couldn't shake the feeling that something bad would happen at any second. His heart began to pound as tightness gripped his chest.

The dog ventured out and came to stand in front of him. He focused on her unusual golden eyes. She looked to be part yellow Labrador retriever and part pointer. Her white-tipped tail wagged slowly. He held out his hand and she sniffed it. It was a shame he didn't have more to feed her. She retreated again and he got in Bethany's buggy.

Inside the small space he started to relax. No one could get behind him now. He glanced at Bethany. She was watching him intently. Could she see how anxious he was? He needed to divert her attention. "Are you waiting for something?"

"Nee." She turned the horse and headed back up the street. The clip-clop of the mare's hooves was muffled by the snow that covered the road. It was the only sound other than the creaking of the buggy. He discovered he would rather hear Bethany's voice.

"What kind of business does the bishop own?"

"Our bishop builds and sells storage sheds as well as farming, but he's thinking of branching out into tiny homes."

"Then he is a progressive fellow?"

"In his business, but our church is a conservative one."

"I noticed a propane tank at your home."

"Our Ordnung allows us to use propane to power business machinery, our refrigerators, washing machines and hot water heaters. We also have running water and indoor bathrooms. We aren't that conservative but our cookstoves and furnaces must use wood or coal."

He glanced out over the dense tree-covered hillsides and the snowcapped mountains in the distance. "It doesn't look like you'll run out of fuel anytime soon as long as you have a strong fellow to chop and haul it."

"My brother does that for me." Her voice was strained. Worry marked her brow with frown lines.

"How old is he?"

"Almost fourteen. Our mother died when Jenny was born. Our father was gone soon afterward." The undertone of bitterness in her voice surprised him.

"So you were raised by your grandparents."

"My grandfather took us in. He was a widower."

"It must've been hard to be both mother and sister to your younger siblings." He found it easier to talk to Bethany than anyone he'd spoken to since the attack. Maybe it was because she talked to cows. He smiled at the memory.

"I never saw caring for my siblings as a burden." She turned the horse off the street into the parking lot surrounded by various sizes of storage sheds.

A tall, muscular Amish fellow stepped away from a half-finished shed and slipped his hammer into a tool belt that hung on his hips. He didn't sport a beard, so Michael knew he wasn't married. His clothes were tattered and sweat-stained, but his smile was friendly as he greeted them. "*Guder mariye*, Bethany. Need a new shed, do you?"

Bethany opened her door but didn't step out. "Good morning, Jesse. Is Bishop Schultz about?"

"*Nee*, he isn't. He's gone to Unity. Their bishop is laid up with pneumonia, and Elmer has gone to do the preaching for their service this Sunday and perform a wedding on Tuesday. He won't be back until Wednesday night."

"Have you seen Ivan today?"

"*Nee*, I've not. Who is that with you?"

"Jesse, this is Michael Shetler. He is a newcomer. He came expecting to work for my grandfather. He hadn't heard about Elijah's passing. I thought perhaps the bishop would know of some work and could find a place for him to stay."

Jesse hooked his thumbs under his suspenders. "There is work aplenty here. You're welcome to bunk on my couch until you can find a place, but you'll have to suffer through my cooking. I'm no hand with a skillet."

Michael got out of the buggy and grabbed his duffel bag. He would rather stay somewhere alone, but he didn't have much choice. He forced a smile and a lighthearted reply. "Your cooking can't be worse than mine. You have yourself a boarder until I can find a place of my own. We can work out the rent later."

"No need for that." Jesse moved to take Michael's bag. "Let me get this for you."

Michael handed it over. Jesse nodded toward the building he had been working on. "If you don't mind, I'd like to finish this shed before taking you out to my place."

"I don't mind. I'll give you a hand with it."

Looking at Michael's cane, Jesse raised one eyebrow. "Are you sure?"

"I can still swing a hammer."

"Then your help will be welcome. I'll see you get paid for the work you do."

"Danki."

Michael turned to Bethany. "Looks like your brother has been granted a reprieve if Jedidiah wasn't able to speak to the bishop."

Bethany's eyes brightened. "That's right."

"Oh, Jedidiah was here and spoke to Elmer before he left," Jesse said cheerfully.

Michael watched the hope fade in her eyes and wished there was something he could do to console her.

Chapter Three

Michael watched Bethany drive away with a sharp unexpected sense of loss. She was a lovely woman, but he sensed she was much more than a pretty face. It was obvious that she cared about her family. Anyone who asked a cow for advice had to have a good sense of humor.

He smiled then quickly pushed thoughts of her out of his head. As much as she intrigued him, he was better off not seeing her.

Forming a relationship with Bethany would mean letting her get close. He couldn't risk that. He had jumped at the chance to come to this part of Maine because it was remote and thinly populated but it held an Amish community. He had left his Amish upbringing once with devastating consequences. After the attack he had returned home hopeful that rejoining his faith and family would repair his shattered life. It hadn't worked out that way. He didn't know what more God needed from him.

Michael's plan for his new life was simple. Live and work alone while coming into contact with as few people as possible. He wasn't a loner by nature. He had become a recluse out of necessity. Avoiding people was the only way he felt safe. The only way he could keep his affliction hidden. Staying with Jesse was risky, but he had nowhere else to go. He could only pray he didn't have an episode in front of him.

A doctor in Philadelphia had called it PTSD. Post-traumatic stress disorder, the result of a robbery gone wrong at the jewelry store where he had worked. What it meant was that his life was no longer his own. He lived in near constant fear. When a full-blown flashback hit he relived every detail as his coworkers, his friends, were killed in front of his eyes. The gunshots, the screams, the sirens—he saw it, heard it, felt it all again just as if it were happening to him the first time.

He never knew when a flashback would happen, making it impossible for him to return to work. Even a walk down a city street left him hearing the footsteps of someone following him, waiting to feel the cold, hard barrel of a gun jammed in his back.

He was the one who had let them in. He was the only one who came out alive. Sometimes he felt he should have died with the others, but he couldn't dwell on that thought. God had other plans for him. He just didn't know what they were.

The heavy thudding of his heart and the sweat on his brow warned him that thinking about it was the last thing he should be doing. He took a deep breath. Concentrate on something else. Think about Bethany asking her cow for advice and the shocked look on her face when she realized he'd heard her conversation. He visualized her in detail as his pulse slowed to a more normal speed.

From the corner of his eye he caught sight of the yellow dog trotting along the edge of the highway in his direction. Did she belong to someone or was she a stray surviving as best she could? Her thin ribs proved she wasn't being cared for if someone did own her. Her chances of surviving the rest of the winter on her own didn't look good. She approached as close as the drive leading into the parking lot. After pacing back and forth a few times she sat down and stared at him.

He turned to Jesse. "Do you know who that dog belongs to?"

Jesse glanced at her and shook his head. "I've seen her around. I think she's a stray."

"Would you happen to have anything I can feed her?"

Jesse laughed. "Are you a softhearted fellow?"

"Is there anything wrong with that if I am?"

"*Nee*, I like animals, too. Maybe more than most people, but I think I'm going to like you, Michael Shetler." Jesse clapped him on the back with his massive hand, almost knocking Michael over. "There's a couple of ham sandwiches in the refrigerator inside the office. You are welcome to them. For you or for the dog. Your choice."

"*Danki.*" Michael walked into a small building with Office in a hand-lettered sign over the door. Inside he found a small refrigerator with a coffeepot sitting on top of it. He took out two of the sandwiches, happy to see they contained thick slices of ham and cheese. After taking a couple of bites from one, he walked out with the rest in his hand. The dog was still sitting in the driveway.

He walked to within a few feet of her and laid the sandwich on the ground. As soon as he moved away she jumped up and gulped down the food. Looking up, she wagged her tail, clearly wanting more.

"Sorry, that's all there is. We are two of a kind, it seems. You needed a handout and so did I. We have Jesse over there to thank for sharing his lunch." Michael chuckled. He had teased Bethany about talking to her cow but here he was talking to a dog. It was too bad Bethany wasn't here to share the joke.

What surprised him was how much he wanted to see her again.

Jeffrey Morgan's home was a little more than a mile farther up the road from Bethany's house. As she pulled in she saw Jeffrey's mother getting out of her car. When she caught sight of Bethany she approached the buggy hesitantly.

"Good afternoon, Mrs. Morgan." Bethany stepped down from the buggy unsure of what to say.

"You are Ivan's mother, aren't you?" The woman remained a few feet away.

"I'm his older sister. Our mother passed away some years ago."

"That's right. Jeffrey told me that. I'm sorry about your grandfather. Jeffrey was fond of him."

"Thank you. Is Jeffrey here?"

"No. He's at school."

"I'm afraid he isn't. I just came from the school. Neither he nor my brother showed up for class today."

Mrs. Morgan looked around fearfully and moved closer to Bethany. "Are you saying that the boys played hooky today?"

"I don't know that word."

"*Hooky?* It means they skipped school without permission."

"Then *ja*, they played hooky."

Mrs. Morgan looked toward the house at the sound of the front door opening. Mr. Morgan stepped out. Jeffrey's mother leaned closer. "Don't tell my husband about this. I will speak to Jeffrey."

Puzzled by her fearful reaction, Bethany nodded. "Please send Ivan home if you see him."

"I will."

Bethany waved to Mr. Morgan. He didn't return the gesture. She got in her buggy and left. Where were those boys and what were they up to?

Bethany arrived home just after noon. She parked the buggy by the barn and stabled her horse. She wasn't any closer to finding her brother or figuring out what he was up to. As she came out of the barn, a car horn sounded. She glanced toward the county road that ran past her lane. Frank Pearson's long white passenger van turned off the blacktop and into her drive. Frank was the pastor of a Mennonite congregation a few miles away. He and her grandfather had become good friends. Frank used to visit weekly for a game of chess and to swap fishing stories.

Frank pulled up beside her and rolled down his window. "Good day, Bethany."

"Hello, Frank. Would you like to come in for some coffee?"

"I'm afraid I don't have time today. I have my bereavement support group meeting in twenty minutes. I just stopped in to see how you're getting along and to invite you and your family to attend one of our meetings when you are ready. It doesn't matter what faith you belong to or even if you are a nonbeliever. We all grieve when we lose loved ones."

"*Danki*, Frank. I don't think it's for me."

"If you change your mind, you're always welcome to join us. Please let me know if you need help with anything. I miss Elijah, but I know my grief is nothing compared to yours. I promised him I'd check in on you."

"Our congregation here is small, but we have been well looked after."

"I'm glad to hear it. I'll stop by again in a few days and stay awhile."

Maybe Frank could reach Ivan. "Why don't you come to dinner on Sunday? I know Ivan and Jenny would enjoy seeing you again. Maybe you can interest Ivan in learning to play chess."

"You know, I believe I will. Your cooking is too good to resist. Thanks for the invite."

"You are always welcome here."

After Frank drove away, Bethany headed for her front door. The smell of warm yeasty dough rising greeted her as she entered the house. Gemma was busy kneading dough at the table. Bethany pulled off her coat and straightened her prayer *kapp*. "What are you doing here again so soon? I thought you said tomorrow?"

"What does it look like I'm doing?"

"It looks like you are making a mess in my kitchen."

Gemma giggled as she surveyed the stack of bowls, pans and the flour-covered table. "It does, doesn't it?" She punched down the dough in a second bowl and dumped it onto a floured tabletop.

"Why are you baking bread in my kitchen?"

"Because you didn't have any. I realized on my way home this morning that the least I could do for a friend was to remedy that."

"I appreciate the gesture but why not bake it at your home and bring the loaves here."

"I didn't want to mess up my kitchen. I just finished washing the floor." Gemma looked at her and winked. "Where have you been, anyway?"

Should she confide in Gemma about Ivan's recent actions and Jedidiah's accusations? Once more Bethany wished her grandfather were still alive. He would know what to do with the boy. She hung her coat on one of the pegs by the kitchen door. "It's a long story."

Gemma looked up. "Oh?"

Bethany went to the far cabinet and pulled out a cup and saucer. She felt the need of some bracing hot tea. "Jedidiah came by earlier. He accused Ivan of stealing two bags of potatoes and a bag of beans from his cellar."

Gemma spun around, outrage written across her face. "He did what?"

"He said Ivan stole those items and he had proof because Ivan sold some of the potatoes to the grocer this morning."

"I don't believe it. I know Ivan has been difficult at times, but he is not a thief."

Bethany filled her cup with hot water from the teakettle on the back of the stove. "That's what I said. I went to the school to hear Ivan's side of the story."

"And?"

"And he wasn't at school. He hasn't been to school all week. He forged a letter from me telling the teacher that he is out sick." Bethany opened a tea bag, added it to her cup and carried it to the kitchen table, where she sat down.

After a long moment of stunned silence, Gemma came to sit across from her. "You poor thing. Still, that doesn't mean he stole from Jedidiah."

"It doesn't prove he didn't. And it certainly doesn't speak well of his character. Jedidiah went straight to Bishop Schultz with the story. I had hoped to speak with the bishop, too, but he is gone to Unity until Wednesday. I don't know how I'll ever convince him to let Ivan remain with us now. What is wrong with my brother? How have I failed him?"

Had Ivan inherited his father's restlessness and his refusal to shoulder his responsibilities? She prayed that wasn't the case.

Gemma reached across the table and laid a comforting hand on Bethany's arm. "I'm so sorry. I had no idea things had progressed to this degree of seriousness. He's always been a little willful, but this is unacceptable behavior and it is his own doing. Bethany, you did not fail him."

"Danki." Bethany appreciated Gemma's attempt to comfort her.

Gemma returned to the other end of the table and began dividing the dough into bread pans. "You'll simply have to talk to the boy and tell him what the bishop has planned. Perhaps that will convince him to mend his ways."

"I hope you are right. Christmas is only five weeks away. I don't know if a change in Ivan's behavior now will be enough to convince Onkel Harvey and the bishop that he should stay with us. Stealing is a serious offense."

Bethany had lost so many people in her family. She couldn't bear the thought of sending her brother away. She had promised to look after her brother and sister and to keep the family together. It felt like she was breaking that promise and it was tearing her heart to pieces.

"You still have the option to marry. I think Jesse would jump at the chance if you gave him any encouragement."

"I saw him this morning and he didn't appear love-struck to me."

Gemma laughed. "Did you honestly go see him with marriage in mind?"

"Of course not. I took a stranger to see the bishop at his workplace. The bishop wasn't there but Jesse was."

"What stranger?" Gemma looked intrigued.

"His name is Michael Shetler. He claims my grandfather offered him a job and a place to stay."

"Did he?"

Bethany shrugged. "I never heard Grandfather mention it."

"What's he like? Is he single?"

"He's rude."

"What does that mean? What did he say to you?" Gemma left the bread dough to rise again and returned to her seat, her eyes alight with eagerness. "Tell me."

Bethany blushed at the memory of Michael listening to her conversation with Clarabelle. That was the last time she would speak to any of the farm animals. "He wasn't actually rude. He simply caught me off guard."

"And?"

"When I told him about Elijah's passing he was very upset. I thought the bishop would be the best person to help him find work, so I gave him a ride to the shed factory. Jesse said he would put him to work."

"You took a stranger up in your buggy? Is he old? Is he cute?"

"He walks with a cane."

"So he's old."

"*Nee.* I'd guess he's twenty-five or so. I had the impression it was a recent injury to his leg."

"So he's young. That's *goot*, but is he nice looking?"

Bethany considered the question. "Michael isn't bad looking. He has a rugged attractiveness."

"Michael?" Gemma tipped her head to the side. "He must be single. Is he someone you'd like to know better?"

"I have too much on my mind to spend time thinking about finding a man."

"That's not much of an answer."

"It's the only answer you are going to get. You'll have the chance to see Mr. Shetler for yourself at the church service next Sunday."

"All right. I won't tease you."

Gemma walked over and put on her coat. "Ivan is a good boy at heart. You know that."

Bethany nodded. "I do. Something is wrong, but I don't know what."

"You'll figure it out. You always do. I'm leaving you with a bit of a mess but all you have to do is put the bread in the oven when it's done rising."

"*Danki*, Gemma. I'm blessed to have you as a friend."

"You would do the same for me. Mamm is planning a big Thanksgiving dinner next Thursday. You and the children are invited of course."

"Tell your mother we'd love to come."

"Invite Michael when you see him again."

"I doubt I'll see him before Sunday next and by then it will be too late."

"My *daed* mentioned the other day he needs a bigger garden shed. Maybe I'll go with him to look at the ones the bishop makes. You aren't going to claim you saw Michael first if I decide I like him, are you?"

Bethany shook her head as she smiled at her friend. "He's all yours."

Bethany was waiting at the kitchen table when both children came home. Ivan sniffed the air appreciatively. "Smells good. Can I have a piece of bread with peanut butter? I'm starved."

Bethany clutched her hands together and laid

them on the table. "After I have finished speaking to you."

"Told you," Jenny said as she took off her coat and boots.

"Talk about what?" Ivan tried to look innocent. Bethany knew him too well. She wasn't fooled.

"Why don't you start by telling me what you did wrong and why." Bethany was pleased that she sounded calm and in control.

"I don't know what you are talking about." He couldn't meet her gaze.

"You do so," Jenny muttered.

"Stay out of this," Ivan snapped.

"I went to school today. I'm not in trouble," Jenny shot back.

"I'm waiting for an explanation, Ivan." Bethany hoped he would own up to his behavior.

"Okay, I skipped school today. It's no big deal. I can make up the work." His defiant tone made her bristle.

"You will make up the work for today, and Thursday and Wednesday and Tuesday. You will also write a letter of apology to your teacher for your deliberate deception. Is there something else you want to tell me?"

He stared at his shoes. "Like what?"

Bethany shook her head. "Ivan, how could you? Skipping school is bad enough. Forging a letter to your teacher is worse yet, but stealing from our neighbors is terrible. I can't believe you would do such a thing. What has gotten into you?"

"Nothing."

"That is not an answer. Why did you steal beans and potatoes from Jedidiah?"

Ivan shrugged. "He has plenty. The Amish are supposed to share what they have with the less fortunate."

"What makes you less fortunate?"

When he didn't answer Bethany drew a deep breath. "Your behavior has shamed us. Worse than that, your actions have been reported to the bishop."

"So? What does the bishop have to do with this?"

"The bishop is responsible for this community," Bethany said. "Because you have behaved in ways contrary to our teachings, the bishop has decided you need more discipline and guidance than I can give you."

"What does that mean?"

"When Onkel Harvey and his family come to visit for Christmas, you will return to Bird-in-Hand with them."

"What? I don't want to live with Onkel Harvey."

"You should've thought about the consequences before getting into so much trouble."

Jenny, who had been standing quietly beside

Ivan, suddenly spoke up. "You're sending him away? Sister, you promised we would all stay together." She looked ready to cry. "You promised."

"This is out of my hands. The bishop and your uncle have decided what Ivan needs. They feel I have insufficient control over you, Ivan. I'm afraid they are right. Bishop Schultz believes you need the firm guidance of a man. If your grandfather was still alive or if I was married, things would be different."

"That's stupid," Ivan said, glaring at Bethany. "I didn't do anything bad enough to be sent away. It isn't fair."

"None of us wants this. You have time before Christmas to change your behavior and convince them to let you stay. You will return the items you've taken from Jedidiah. He knows that you sold one of the bags of potatoes you took. You must give the money you received for them to Jedidiah. You will have to catch up on all your missed schoolwork and behave politely to Jedidiah and to the bishop. We will pray that your improvement is enough to convince Bishop and Onkel Harvey to let you remain with us."

Ivan glared at her. "Jedidiah Zook is a creep. He's never nice to me, so why should I be nice to him?"

Bethany planted her hands on her hips. "That attitude is exactly what got you into this mess."

Jenny wrapped her arms around her brother's waist. "I don't want you to go away. I'll tell the bishop you'll be good."

"They don't care what we think because we're just kids and we don't count."

"That's enough, Ivan. You and I will go now to speak to Jedidiah and return his belongings this evening."

"I can't."

"What do you mean that you can't?"

He shrugged. "I don't have the stuff or the money anymore. I gave it away."

"Who did you give it to?" Bethany asked.

"I don't have to tell you." He pushed Jenny away and rushed through the house and out the back door. Bethany followed, shouting after him, but he ran into the woods at the back of the property and disappeared from her view.

Jenny began crying. Bethany picked her up to console her. Jenny buried her face in the curve of Bethany's neck. "You can't send him away. You can't. Do something, sister."

"I will try, Jenny. I promise I will try."

Ivan returned an hour later. Not knowing what else to do, Bethany sent him to bed without supper. Jenny barely touched her meal. Bethany didn't have an appetite, either. She wrote out a check to Jedidiah for the value of the stolen items and put it in an envelope with a brief letter of apology. She couldn't face him in person.

After both children were in bed, Bethany stood in front of the door to her grandfather's workshop. He wouldn't be in there but she hoped that she could draw comfort from the things he loved. She pushed open the door.

Moonlight reflecting off the snow outside cast a large rectangle of light through the window. It fell across his desk and empty chair. She walked to the chair and laid her hands on the back of it. The wood was cold beneath her fingers. She closed her eyes and drew a deep breath. The smell of the oils he used, the old leather chair and the cleaning rag that was still lying on the desk brought his beloved face into sharp focus. Tears slipped from beneath her closed eyelids and ran down her cheeks. She wiped them away with both hands.

"I miss you, Daadi. We all miss you. I know you are happy with our Lord in heaven and with Mammi and Mamm. That gives me comfort, but I still miss you." Her voice sounded odd in the empty room.

Opening her eyes, she sat in his chair and lit the lamp. The pieces of a watch lay on the white felt-covered board he worked on. His tiny screwdrivers and tools were lined up neatly in their case. Everything was just as it had been the last time he sat in this chair. The cleaning rag was the only thing out of place. She picked it up to return it to the proper drawer and saw an envelope lying beneath it. It was unopened. The name on the return address caught her attention. It was from Michael Shetler of Sugarcreek, Ohio.

Chapter Four

"Why didn't you tell me that you repair watches?"

Michael looked up from Jesse's table saw. Bethany stood in the workshop's doorway he had left open to take advantage of the unusually warm afternoon. She stood with her hands on her hips and a scowl on her pretty face.

The mutt, lying in the rectangle of sunlight, had already alerted him that someone was coming with a soft woof. She shot outside and around the corner of the building. The sight of Bethany made Michael want to smile. She was every bit as appealing as he remembered, even with a slight frown marring her face.

He pushed away his interest. Jesse had filled in a lot of details about the family last night. Bethany was trying to keep her family together. Jesse said without her grandfather and her brother to work the farm she could lose it. A handsome woman in need of help was trouble and Michael had enough trouble. He positioned the two-by-four length of pine board and made the cut. As the saw blade quit spinning he took the board and added it to the stack on his right. He kept his face carefully blank when he met her gaze. "I didn't think it would make a difference."

"It certainly would have."

"How so? Your grandfather is gone. You said you couldn't afford to hire help."

"You neglected to tell me you had sent the first and last months' rent on the cabin."

He picked up another board and settled it in the slot he had created for the correct length so he didn't have to measure and mark each piece of wood. Bishop Schultz used a diesel generator to supply electricity inside his carpentry shop. The smell of fresh sawdust mixed with diesel fumes that drifted through the open door. Michael squeezed the trigger on the saw and lowered the blade. It sliced through the pine board in two seconds, spewing more sawdust on the growing pile beneath the table.

He tossed the cut wood on the stack and reached for another two-by-four. Bethany crossed the room and took hold of the board before he could position it. "Why didn't you tell me you had already paid the rent?"

"I figured you would mention it if you knew

about it. Since you didn't say anything and you already had a crisis to deal with, I thought it could wait for a better time."

"That was very considerate of you. A better time is right now. My grandfather never deposited your check. In fact, he never read your last letter. I only found it yesterday evening."

She let go of his board and reached into a small bag she carried over her arm. "I have the check here. I've been unable to bring myself to clean out his workshop. For that reason, his agreement with you went undiscovered." She held out the check. He didn't take it.

"Do you know the rest of your grandfather's offer?" He kept his gaze averted.

"Your letter said you agreed to work with him for six months. Was there more?"

"If he considered me skillful enough after that time he would make me a fifty-fifty partner in the business." He looked at her. "I can show you his offer in writing if you want to see it."

"There's no need. I believe you. Are you still willing to do that?"

"How can I be a partner now that he is gone?"

"The business belongs to me but I can't repair watches, so it is worthless except for his tools. I had planned to sell them unless Ivan showed an interest in learning the trade."

"Has he?"

"Not yet."

"How is the boy?" he asked softly.

A wry smile lifted the corner of her mouth. "I wish I knew. Right now he seems mad at the world."

"Boys grow up. He'll come around."

"I pray you are right. I have a proposition for you, Mr. Shetler."

"Call me Michael."

She smiled and nodded once. "Michael. It's similar to the one my grandfather offered you. Work for me for six months. You keep two-thirds of everything you earn during that time. I will keep one-third as rent on the shop, for the use of Grandfather's client list and his tools. If at the end of that time I am satisfied with your skill I will sell you the business or we can continue as partners."

"Who is to decide if my skills are adequate?"

"My grandfather did the majority of his work for a man named George Meyers in Philadelphia. He owns a jewelry shop and watch repair business. If Mr. Meyers is satisfied with the quality of work you do, then that is all the assurance I need."

Michael smiled inwardly. One part of the puzzle had finally been solved. George had started this whole thing. It was certainly like George, to go out of his way for someone who didn't deserve the kindness. Michael wondered how much, if anything, George had shared about his condition with Bethany's grandfather. "I wondered how your grandfather got my name. Now I know."

"I'm afraid I don't follow you."

"I used to work for George Meyers." Up until the night he had let two armed criminals into the business George owned.

"Why did you quit? Is that when you got hurt?"

His heart started pounding like a hammer inside his chest as the onset of a panic attack began. In another minute he would be on the ground gasping for air. He wasn't about to recount the horrors he saw that night to Bethany. He had to get outside. "I don't like to talk about it."

He grabbed an armful of cut wood and pushed past Bethany. "Jesse is going to wonder what's keeping me."

She followed him outside. "I'm sorry if it seemed that I was prying. If you don't want to work for me, I understand, but the cabin is still yours for two months."

"I'll think about the job, but I'll take the cabin." He kept walking. It wasn't that he wanted to be rude but he needed her to leave. His anxiety was rising rapidly.

"The cabin is yours whenever you want."

The yellow dog came around the side of the building and launched herself at him. He side-stepped to keep from being hit with her muddy paws. One of the boards slid out of his arms. "Down."

She dropped to her belly and barked once, then rolled over, inviting him to scratch her muddy stomach.

"I see you still have your friend," Bethany said, humor bubbling beneath her words.

He looked from her to the dog. "I don't have anything to feed you, mutt, unless you eat two-by-fours."

The dog jumped to her feet, picked up the board he had dropped and took off with it in her mouth.

"Hey, bring that back!"

The dog made a sweeping turn and raced back, splashing through puddles of melted snow. She came to a stop and sat in front of him, holding the four-foot length of wood like a prized bone.

"Goot hund." He reached for the board but the dog took off before he touched it. She made a wild run between the sheds lined up at the edge of the property where the snow was still deep.

Bethany burst out laughing. "Good dog, indeed."

He liked the sound of her laughter. The heaviness in his chest dissipated and he grinned. "It seems her previous owner didn't spend much time training her."

"I can see that. She is friendlier since she's had a few meals. She seems to have a lot of puppy in her yet. In a way she reminds me of my brother."

"How so?"

"A lot of potential, but very little focus."

"I'd like to meet this kid."

"I'm sure you will since you'll be living just out our back door."

He frowned. "The cabin is close to your house?"

"Fifty yards, maybe less."

"I assumed it was more secluded."

"It is set back in the woods. We won't bother you if that's what you are worried about."

"I like my privacy." He couldn't very well explain he was worried she'd hear him yelling in the middle of the night.

The dog came trotting back and sat down between them, still holding her trophy. Michael bent to grab the board as Bethany did the same. They smacked heads. His hat flipped off and landed in the snow. The dog dropped the wood, snatched up the hat and took off with it.

Michael held his head and glanced at Bethany. "Are you okay?"

Bethany rubbed her smarting forehead. Maybe it was a sign that she needed some sense knocked into her. She had come to give Michael his money back and had ended up offering him a job instead. The thump on her skull had come too late. "I'm fine."

"Are you sure? Do you want some ice?"

"*Nee*, it won't leave a mark. Will it?" She pulled her hand away.

He bent closer. "I think you're going to have a bump."

"Great."

"I am sorry." He looked down at the dog, now standing a few feet away, still holding his hat. "See what you did to Bethany."

The dog whined and lay down, the picture of dejection. Bethany crouched and offered her hand to the animal. "Don't scold the poor thing. It wasn't her fault. Are you going to keep her?"

"I can't walk away and leave her to fend for herself. Besides, her goofy behavior leaves me smiling more often than not. *Ja*, I will keep her. She seems to have decided she belongs with me."

Bethany knew she should leave but found herself reluctant to go. There was something intriguing about the man. One minute they were discussing his job and the next second he went pale as a sheet and couldn't get away from her fast enough. A few minutes later they were both laughing at the antics of a stray dog. The truth was she liked him. A lot. But she had to find a way to keep her family together. She couldn't allow a distraction to interfere with that.

She took the hat from the dog and handed it to Michael. "I should get going."

"Right." He nodded but didn't move.

She took a few steps toward her buggy but something made her turn around. He was still watching her. "Michael, do you play chess?"

"I enjoy the game. Why?"

"Would you do me a favor?"

"If I can."

"I have a friend of my grandfather coming to supper on Sunday evening. He and Daadi used to play chess every week. I know he misses Daadi and their games. I don't play. If you aren't doing anything, would you like to join us for supper and give Pastor Frank a game or two?"

Hadn't she just decided she didn't need a distraction? Maybe he would say no. "Don't feel obligated just because I asked."

"I need to get moved in. I'm not sure I'll find the time."

"You have to eat."

"Another time maybe."

"Of course." She turned away, more disappointed than she cared to admit.

"Bethany?"

"Ja?" She spun around hopefully.

"I appreciate the job offer. I'll give it some serious thought. Do I get the key to the cabin from you?"

"It isn't locked. You'll find the key hanging on a nail just inside the door. When you come to my place you'll see a wooded ridge behind the house. The cabin is up there. Just follow the lane. Do you have transportation? I can send Ivan to pick you up."

"Jesse has offered me the loan of a pony and cart until I can send for my horses. Is there someone locally who sells buggies?"

"There's a carriage maker in Unity. I've heard he is reasonable."

"I'll look into it."

"If you change your mind about having supper with us tomorrow night, just show up. There will be plenty to eat."

"Are you a *goot* cook?"

She grinned. "Do you expect a modest Amish woman to brag on herself?"

"I expect a modest Amish woman to tell the truth."

She bobbed her head once. "I could tell you that I'm a very good cook, but I suggest you come to supper and decide for yourself."

After stepping up into her buggy, she looked back and saw he was still watching her. A tingle of pleasure at his interest lifted her spirits. Just as quickly, she dismissed her feeling as foolishness. Her mother's unhappy life spent loving the wrong kind of man had driven home to Bethany just how cruel romantic love could be. She was determined not to suffer the same way. If she married it would be a beneficial arrangement based on sound judgment. Not love. She waved and then drove away. Would Michael come or wouldn't he? She would have to wait an entire day to find out.

Jesse walked past Michael with a load of boards in his arms. "Have you decided to hang on to her or are you going to ignore her and hope she goes away?"

Michael scowled at him. "What does that mean?"

Jesse stopped and gave Michael a funny look. "I was just wondering if you are planning to keep the dog. What did you think I meant?"

Relieved that he wasn't referring to Bethany, Michael decided to share the joke. "Bethany Martin was just here."

Jesse chuckled. "I wouldn't tell a fella to ignore Bethany and hope she goes away, but the same can't be said for some other single women in this community."

Although Jesse hadn't made Bethany's wish list when she had been talking to the cow about walking out with someone, Michael liked the man and thought he would make a decent husband. "Do you have your eye on one maid in particular?"

"Me? *Nee*, I'm not ready to get into harness

with any female. They talk too much, and they expect you to talk back to them. I don't have that much to say. I can't imagine a lifetime of staring at a woman who is waiting for me to utter something interesting. If you are looking to go courting, Bethany Martin is a fine woman. You wouldn't be stepping on anyone's toes."

"I'm not interested in courting, but I did wonder why she isn't already married."

"Her grandfather told me that she wants to get her brother and sister raised before she looks to start another family."

"Did you know Elijah well?"

"He was a fine friend. Everyone loved him. He was always laughing, quick with a joke, always ready to lend a helping hand. It didn't matter if you were Amish or not. There are only twenty adult members in this church, six *youngees* and five *kinder*. We know each other well."

Youngees were unmarried teens in their running around time or *rumspringa*. The potential marriage pool in the community was small indeed. Bethany would have to look for a marriage partner farther afield if Jesse or Jedidiah didn't work out.

Michael couldn't seem to curb his curiosity about her and her family. "What's the story with her brother?"

Jesse was silent for a long moment. "I'm not one to speak ill of another."

"I'm sorry. I wasn't looking for gossip. I can form my own opinion of the family. You don't have to say anything."

"It's not that. We are newcomers to this area. Bethany and her family have been here the longest. Two years now. I came sixteen months ago. Jedidiah and the other families came after I did. We get along with the *Englisch* and for the most part they get along with us. There are a few exceptions. People who would like to see us leave. When something goes wrong, those few are quick to point to the Amish and say it must be our fault. Ivan has been a mischief maker for as long as I've known him, but I don't believe all that is said against him these days."

"You think he is getting blamed for what someone else is doing?"

Jesse stared into the distance for a long minute, and then he looked Michael in the eye. "I think he makes an easy target."

Michael considered Jesse's carefully worded reply. "What does the bishop think?"

"He hasn't confided in me. I should get back to work. I don't want him to think I slack off when he's gone. Oh, and I meant to tell you I've got some extra nylon webbing if you want to fashion a collar for your mutt. What did Bethany want, anyway?"

Michael followed Jesse to the skeleton of the shed he was putting up. "She discovered her grandfather did rent a cabin to me. She found my rent check last night. She came to give me a choice of getting my money back or staying on the property."

"So, am I losing you as a roommate already?"

"You are. I'll leave tomorrow."

"*Goot.* That makes you the best kind of house-guest."

Michael glanced his way. "What kind is that?"

"One who leaves before he has worn out his welcome." Jesse grinned and clapped Michael on the back then pulled his hammer from his tool belt and went to work.

Michael relaxed. He laid down the boards he'd cut and walked back to the workshop. He thought getting a few answers about Bethany would appease his curiosity but he had been mistaken. It seemed it wasn't so easy to put her out of his mind.

Maybe he'd made a mistake telling her he still wanted to rent the cabin. How was he going to stop thinking about her if he lived fifty yards from her home? If he took the job she was going to be his boss.

He would have to discourage her from visiting

the workshop. He worked best alone and he liked it that way. That was the reason he had come to Maine. She would just have to learn to accept it.

Bethany opened the oven to check her peach pie and decided it was done. The crust was golden brown and the juices were bubbling up between the lattice strips. She pulled it out and placed it on the cooling rack at the end of the counter. She then lifted the lid on the pot of chili and sniffed the mouthwatering aroma. Using a spoon, she scooped up a sample and blew on it before tasting it. The deep, rich, spicy flavor was delicious but it needed a touch more salt. After adding two shakes, she stirred the pot and replaced the lid. All she needed now was the rest of her company.

Would Michael come? She hoped he would.

"It smells *wunderbar*," Gemma said as she set the plates on the table.

"Let's hope it tastes as good as it smells." Bethany walked to the window that overlooked the path up to the cabin. She had invited Gemma to join them as a defense against her attraction to Michael. Gemma's lighthearted and flirty ways were sure to liven the evening and keep Michael entertained.

"Any sign of him?"

Bethany dropped the window shade. "Any sign of who?"

"The person you're hoping to see. You realize you've been to that window ten times in the last thirty minutes. I can't imagine that you are this anxious to catch sight of Pastor Frank. Therefore, it must be someone else. I'm going to take a wild guess and say it is a man. A newcomer. Someone who walks with a cane." She raised one eyebrow at Bethany. "Am I close?"

"If you must know, I did invite Michael Shetler. He plays chess and I know that Pastor Frank misses the games he used to have with Elijah."

"That was very thoughtful of you. Why am I here? I don't play chess."

"You're here because I didn't want it to look like I had invited Michael for personal reasons. You know what I mean."

"You didn't want him to think you were angling for a return date? Or were you hoping I would catch his interest?"

"Both. When he sees I invited a single woman from our community to join us, he won't think I have designs on him myself."

A sly grin curved Gemma's lips. "What if this backfires and he *does* like me better?"

"Then I will be happy for both of you and you can name your first daughter after me."

Gemma laughed and returned to setting the table. Bethany resisted the urge to look out the window again. It was possible Michael had made his way to the cabin without her seeing him, but she hoped he would at least stop by and let her know he had taken possession.

The rumble of a car announced the arrival of Pastor Frank. Bethany went to the front door to greet him and saw Michael turning in from the highway in a small cart pulled by a black-and-white pony. To her chagrin, he simply waved and went past the house on the track that led to the cabin. She tried not to let her disappointment show. She stepped aside to allow Frank to enter the house and closed the door against the chilly afternoon. It was clear Michael wasn't eager to see her again.

After seeing Bethany's smile fade when he drove past her home, Michael almost changed his mind and went back. Almost. His best course of action was to see as little of her as possible. Out of sight, out of mind. He hoped. While he found her attractive, he couldn't offer her anything but a business partnership. To encourage anything else would be grossly unfair.

The cabin he had rented was set back in a small grove of trees up the hillside behind her place. As she had promised, the road up to it was well marked and had been plowed recently.

A small weathered barn came with the cabin and he stopped Jesse's pony beside it. A quick tour proved it would be enough for his two buggy horses and his buggy when he got one. The only drawback to the property was the steep hillside behind the barn. With his bum leg he'd never be able to get down to the bottom and lead his horses back up when he turned them out to pasture in the summer. He unharnessed the pony and led him inside to a roomy stall. Jesse had supplied Michael with enough hay and horse chow to last him a week.

He moved the horse feed inside and left the hay in the back of the small wagon. He was thankful to see a water pump stood near the barn. It would make keeping the animals watered easier even in the winter.

As he was heading to the cabin with his duffel bag over his shoulder, he saw the dog come trotting up the road. She had followed him from town as he'd hoped she would. He had tried to coax her into the cart, but she'd refused to have anything to do with it even after he lifted her into the bed. "You're a good girl. I'm glad to see you made it."

She ignored him and went to explore in the barn. Michael put his bag down on the porch and tried to open the door. It was locked. He was sure Bethany had told him it would be unlocked. He tried again to make sure the door wasn't just stuck but it wasn't.

He made his way to the back door with difficulty. The snow was deep enough in places to leave him unsure of his footing. If not for his cane and the wall of the cabin, he would have fallen several times. After all his struggles he found the back door was locked, as well. He could see that it had been opened recently by the arch of snow that had been pushed aside. A trail of footprints led from the stoop up the hill into woods. They were small footprints, those of a woman or a child.

Making his way back to the front porch was easier. The dog was sitting by the door waiting for him. He looked at the house below him on the hillside. It seemed he would have to face Bethany after all to get the key. He made his way down the road and knocked on her front door.

Chapter Five

The moment Bethany opened her door Michael knew he was in trouble. Her bright smile and the eagerness in her eyes pushed at the mental wall he had erected to keep people from getting too close.

He didn't want to shut her out. He wanted to be worthy of the friendliness she seemed so willing to share.

"You have decided to join us, after all. Come in, Michael. Please have a seat." She stepped aside and gestured for him to enter.

He shook his head. "I'm not here to eat."

Disappointment replaced the eagerness in her eyes. "Oh? What can I do for you, then?"

She moved back and he stepped inside. The dog squeezed in to stay at his side. Bethany frowned slightly but didn't say anything.

The house was typical of the Amish houses

he'd seen all his life. From the entryway a door to his right led directly into the kitchen. Beautiful pine cabinets lined the walls. The floor was covered with a checkerboard pattern of black-and-white linoleum. The windows had simple white pull-down shades instead of curtains. The delicious aromas of Bethany's home-cooked meal filled the air. His stomach growled.

He resisted the urge to stay and make her smile again. "The cabin is locked. I can't get in."

Bethany cocked her head slightly. "Are you sure? Maybe the door is just stuck."

"I'm sure. The back door is locked, too."

"Why does he need in the cabin?" Ivan demanded, scowling at Michael.

Bethany gave her brother a sharp look. "Michael is going to be living there. Daadi rented the place to him. Do you know anything about the cabin being locked?"

"I don't know why you're asking me," Ivan snapped. "Every time something goes wrong I get blamed." He pushed to his feet and rushed out of the room.

Color blossomed in Bethany's cheeks as she glanced at her guests. "I apologize for Ivan's behavior. I thought he was doing better. Jenny, did you lock the cabin?"

Jenny shook her head, making the ribbons of her *kapp* dance on her shoulders. "I play there sometimes with Ivan and Jeffrey, but I didn't lock the door."

Bethany met Michael's gaze but quickly looked away. "I believe there is a spare key in Grandfather's bedroom. If you'll excuse me, I'll go find it. It may take me a moment or two. I'm not sure where Daadi kept it."

The dog suddenly left Michael's side. He made a grab for her and missed. "Mutt, get back here."

She ignored him and went to investigate the new people in the room. She gave the young Amish woman and the *Englisch* fellow at the table a brief sniff, then rounded the far end. Jenny had her hands out. The dog settled her head in Jenny's lap and looked up with soulful adoring eyes as the girl scratched her behind her ears.

"What a beautiful dog." Jenny stroked her soft fur. "I think she likes me."

Michael walked over and took hold of a length of black nylon webbing Jesse had fashioned into a makeshift collar. "I'm afraid she hasn't learned any manners."

"What's her name?" Jenny asked.

"Mutt." He still wasn't sure he would keep her, although she seemed to have attached herself to him. Maybe she would like Jenny better and stay here.

The slender man in *Englisch* clothing rose to his feet. "Mutt is not much of a name but it's better than Cat. I'm Pastor Frank Pearson. You can call me Frank." He swept a hand toward the young Amish woman seated across from him. "This is Bethany's friend Gemma Lapp and you must be Michael Shetler."

The pastor held out his hand. Meeting new people made Michael uneasy. He rubbed his sweaty palm on his pant leg before taking the man's hand in a firm grip. "I take it you are the chess player."

Frank's expression brightened. "I am. Do you play?"

"Now and again."

"We'll have to arrange a match someday. I'm sorry you didn't get to meet Elijah. He was a true master of the game. He told me quite a bit about you."

Michael grew cold. "Is that so? I don't know what he could have told you. We never met."

The pastor's expression didn't change. "He said you came highly recommended by an old friend of his. I believe it was George Meyers and that you grew up near Sugarcreek in Ohio. My grandmother was from the Sugarcreek area, but she left many years ago. Please, have a seat."

It had been a long day and Michael just wanted to get settled in a place of his own. He accepted the invitation mainly because his leg was aching.

"Would you like some *kaffi*?" Gemma asked.

He nodded. She rose and brought him a cup

and saucer with three pale yellow cookies on the plate. "These are lemon crinkles. My specialty. I hope you like them."

"Danki." The coffee was black and bracing. The cookies were light, tart and delicious.

"You can't call her Mutt," Jenny said from the other end of the table.

"Why don't you name her?" Gemma suggested.

Jenny peered into the dog's eyes. "I'm going to call you Sadie Sue. Do you like that name?"

The dog barked once and everyone laughed.

"That settles it," Michael said. "She is now and forever Sadie Sue."

"How are the cookies?" Gemma gave Michael a smile every bit as sweet as the pastry.

"They're delicious. They remind me of the ones my grandmother used to make." He prayed Bethany would hurry up before he was subjected to more questions. She came back in the room a few seconds later.

"Found it." She held the key aloft.

Michael grimaced as he stood and leaned heavily on the table. He had been sitting just long enough for his leg to stiffen. When the sharp pain subsided he picked up his cane.

"Are you all right?" Bethany asked, reaching a hand toward him.

Her sympathy irritated him. He hated when

people treated him as if they expected him to topple over at any second. "I'm fine."

"How were you injured?" Gemma asked softly.

His throat tightened. He couldn't draw a full breath. The walls of the house started to close in. He needed to get outside. "I've got to get going."

He saw the confusion in Bethany's eyes, but nothing mattered except getting enough air. He pushed past her and went out the door. On the porch he stopped to scan the yard and outbuildings for signs of danger. Was someone lurking in the woods beyond the road? He took a step to the side and backed up to the wall of the house so that no one could get behind him. Sadie followed him out and sat at his side, nuzzling his hand. He stroked her head.

After a few deep breaths of the cold air, Michael's panic receded. It was okay. There wasn't any danger. He took one step away from the safety of Bethany's house and then another, glad to escape without having her watch him fall apart.

Gemma propped her elbow on the table with her chin in her hand. "Did that seem odd to anyone else?"

Bethany had to admit Gemma was right. "He acted like he couldn't get out of here fast enough."

"I hope it wasn't my cookies." Gemma sat back and folded her arms across her chest.

Pastor Frank took a sip of his coffee. "I don't think it was anything we said or did. Michael has been through a rough time."

Bethany turned to Frank. "What do you know about him?"

"Only a few things that your grandfather shared with me. I don't feel it's my place to repeat what was said."

Gemma arched one eyebrow. "Okay, now you've made me curious."

Frank smiled but he shook his head. "Many people tell me things in confidence. I take that responsibility seriously. I think it's enough to say that Michael came to New Covenant seeking privacy and a chance to heal in body and mind."

"Is there anything we can do for him?" Bethany asked.

"We can invite him to our Thanksgiving dinner," Gemma suggested. "He shouldn't spend the holiday alone."

Pastor Frank nodded. "Good idea. Treat him like you would anyone else. Be friendly, be kind, be compassionate, don't pry. I suspect he will discover soon enough if he truly belongs here."

Gemma rolled her eyes. "One winter was enough to convince me I didn't belong here. I don't mind snow, but when it gets so deep you can't see the cows standing out in it, that's too much snow."

Bethany chuckled. "And yet here you are facing another winter in northern Maine."

"I can't. What would you do without me?"

"I honestly don't know," Bethany admitted. Gemma was a dear friend and she would miss her terribly if she ever left New Covenant.

"Gemma, will you serve the peach pie and ice cream for me? I must speak with Ivan. His behavior tonight was not acceptable." Bethany braced herself for a verbal battle with Ivan as she climbed the stairs to his bedroom. She knocked softly. He didn't answer.

She opened the door and discovered he wasn't in his room. Her conversation with him would have to wait but it would take place. He wasn't getting out of it this easily. She checked the other rooms and the attic, knowing he sometimes liked to hide in those places, but she didn't find him.

When Bethany came downstairs she joined the others and enjoyed a slice of pie and ice cream. When everyone was finished, Gemma began clearing the table.

Pastor Frank patted his stomach. "That was a very good meal. Invite me more often, Bethany."

She summoned a smile. "Come anytime. I'll feed you."

He laughed as he rose and got ready to leave. She handed him his gloves after he finished buttoning his coat. "I'm glad you came tonight, Frank. We have missed your company."

"I'm glad I came, too. What did Ivan have to say for himself?"

She clasped her hands together. "He wasn't in his room. He must have slipped out the back door. What am I going to do with him?"

"He's a troubled boy. All you can do is show him you care about him, give him the opportunity to confide in you and pray he finds the courage to tell you what's bothering him."

"I know he doesn't want to be sent to live with our uncle. I had hoped learning that he only has until Christmas to mend his ways would be incentive enough."

"Unfortunately, it may only add to the pressure he's under."

"Will you talk to him?"

"As a family friend or in my official capacity as a psychologist? Would your bishop approve of that?"

Bethany squeezed her fingers together tightly. She wasn't sure but she was willing to risk more of the bishop's disapproval. "I think he would allow it but I'm asking as a friend."

"Then I will be happy to see Ivan. Bring him by my home any day after school this week. If he'll come."

"I will do that."

He started out the door but stopped and looked back. "One more thing. Will you give a message to Michael Shetler for me?"

"Of course."

"Tell him my door is always open if he needs someone to talk to. That's all. Good night."

"I'll tell him. Good night, Frank." Bethany closed the door behind him. What did Frank know about Michael's past that he felt he couldn't share with her?

Michael unlocked the front door of the cabin and stepped inside. Instantly he knew someone had been there before him. The back door was open a crack. He was sure it had been locked earlier. He crossed the room and closed the door, uneasy at the thought of someone having access. His anxiety level climbed as he thought about trying to sleep in an unsecured place. He thanked God for the dog at his side. A dead bolt and new locks for the doors were a must first thing in the morning.

The dog stayed by his side as he searched the building. Her calm attitude reassured him that the visitor was long gone. The place was neat and cozy. The cabin was a single room with a tiny kitchen in one corner. A bump out beyond the kitchen contained a modern bathroom with a shower and a propane hot water heater. Two big windows on the south wall let in plenty of evening light. A metal bed frame in the far corner held a bare mattress with a sleeping bag on it. A glance around the room gave him the impression that someone visited often. There were empty food wrappers and several magazines beside the fireplace. Perhaps Ivan and Jenny played here. He walked back to pick up his bag near the front door.

Glass shattered, startling him. Michael saw two boys through the broken window before his leg gave out and he hit the floor. Instantly, he was back in the jewelry store, in the middle of the robbery. He had to get out. He crawled toward the door and pulled it open, expecting another bullet. Someone was screaming. Sirens grew closer. Red lights flashed on the ceiling overhead. The smell of gunpowder choked him.

A dog started barking. There hadn't been a dog there that night. He tried to concentrate on the sound. The dog was real. The rest was a nightmare, so realistic he could hear the robbers' voices, he could see their mask-covered faces, he felt the impact of the bullet and the burning pain in his leg. He kept crawling to get away from them.

"Mister, are you okay?"

The new voice, like the barking dog, wasn't a part of the past. Michael struggled to focus on it.

Bethany's brother was kneeling beside him. He didn't want anybody to see him like this. "Go away."

"I'm going to go get help." The boy jumped to his feet and ran toward the house down the hill. Michael crawled after Ivan but couldn't stop him.

Not Bethany. Don't bring Bethany.

It was his last thought before the nightmare sucked him back into the past and made him relive the unbearable. He screamed in pain as a bullet shattered his thigh. He wept as his coworkers were murdered one by one. The wail of sirens grew louder. He knew he was next.

"Michael, can you hear me?"

Another voice not from the past.

"Don't shoot," Michael begged, but the gunshots came again and again. He jerked each time.

"Can you tell me what's wrong? Are you hurt?" The different voice was insistent. Michael tried to hold on to it. He reached out his hand. Someone took hold of it.

"It's Pastor Frank Pearson. We just met. What's wrong, Michael?"

"He's killing them. He's killing them all. Don't shoot."

"Michael, I want you to listen to me. You're safe. No one is shooting. You're in Bethany's cabin in Maine. No one can hurt you here. You're safe. Michael, you're safe."

"I'm in Maine." Harsh panting filled his ears. He knew he was making that sound but he couldn't stop.

"I want you to listen to my voice. No one is hurting you."

Michael turned his head and tried to focus on the man kneeling beside him. He wanted out of this nightmare, but he didn't know how. "Help."

"I'm here to help you. I think you are having a flashback to something bad that happened before. It's not happening now. It's all in the past. Do you understand? You are safe. No one will hurt you."

Michael had no idea how long he lay on the snowy ground listening to Pastor Frank's voice, but slowly the cold air began penetrating the nightmare. The cold was now. The cold was the present. He took a deep breath and then another. He was looking up at darkening sky. There was a single white cloud drifting overhead. It looked like a catcher's mitt. He heard soft whining. Turning his head slowly, he focused on Sadie Sue. She lay beside him with her head on his thigh.

Michael's pounding heart began to slow. He laid a hand on her head. *"Goot hund."*

"Are you feeling better?" Pastor Frank was still kneeling at Michael's side.

Embarrassed that anyone had seen him like this, Michael struggled to sit up. "I'm fine."

"I'm glad to hear that. If you would like to

tell me about what happened, I will be happy to listen."

"I don't want to talk about it." Michael struggled to get up. Pastor Frank gave him a hand and helped him to his feet.

"That's perfectly understandable."

Michael looked around. "Where is my cane?"

Sadie sat at his side, her wagging tail sweeping the snow from his doorstep. She leaned against him as he patted her head.

Pastor Frank located Michael's cane inside the door and handed it to him. He smiled at the dog. "The Lord provides comfort for us in many amazing ways."

Michael wanted nothing more than to retreat inside the cabin and lock the door. "Thanks for the help. I was fortunate I fell at your feet."

"Actually, you didn't. You fell at Ivan's feet. I had just finished having supper with Gemma and Bethany. I was getting in my van when Ivan raced up and said you needed help."

Ivan was standing a few yards away from them. His pale face and wide eyes revealed how frightened he was. Michael rubbed his hands together to warm them. "I'm sorry I scared you, Ivan."

"You may have done more good than harm," Frank said softly and beckoned Ivan closer. "He insists he was the one who threw a rock through your window, but I have my doubts."

"I saw two figures," Michael said.

Ivan approached slowly. "I thought you had been hit in the head or something. I thought you were dying."

Michael managed a half smile. "As you can see, I'm not."

"Why did you break the window?" Frank asked.

Ivan stared at the ground and shifted from one foot to the other. "I don't know."

"I think you do," Frank said.

"Jeffrey and I like to hang out here. We were mad that we couldn't use it as a meeting place anymore. I guess we thought you might not stay if the window was broken. We didn't mean to hurt you."

"Actions have consequences," Frank said sternly. "Your wrath served no good purpose. Before you act in anger again, you must think about this day."

"I will. Are you going to tell Bethany about this?"

"No," Michael said emphatically.

Frank placed a hand on Ivan's shoulder. "You'd better go home. Your sister was looking for you."

"To scold me again, right?"

"To talk to you about what's really bothering you. Your sister loves you. You know that."

"Sure, that's why she's sending me away." The

boy turned and walked toward the house with lagging steps.

"He's got a chip on his shoulder," Michael said.

"He does, but right now I'm more concerned about you."

Michael grew uncomfortable under Frank's intense scrutiny. "I told you I'm fine."

"How often do you have these flashbacks?"

"I don't know what you're talking about."

"Yes, you do. Why deny it? What's important is that I know exactly what you are going through. I used to be in your shoes. I dealt with PTSD for three years before my symptoms improved. I haven't had a flashback for five years now."

"How?"

"How did I get better? Time and therapy. Why don't we step inside out of the cold?"

Michael limped into the cabin. The dog followed him in and went to lie in front of the fireplace.

"I don't have much in the way of furniture yet. I'm having some stuff shipped from home." There was an overstuffed green leather chair by the fireplace and two straight-backed chairs that came with the cabin. Michael lowered himself into the upholstered chair and glanced at Frank. "What caused your PTSD?"

Frank turned one of the wooden chairs around

and straddled it. "I served in the military right out of high school. I saw some brutal fighting and horrible situations at a very young age. I married while I was in the service. I thought I was tough. I thought I was okay but a few months after I got home I started having episodes where I re-lived the most frightening events I went through. I started having nightmares, panic attacks. I be-came moody, bitter and depressed. My wife didn't know how to deal with me, and we divorced. Thankfully a fellow veteran recognized what was wrong with me and got me help."

"You stopped having them?" Michael wanted desperately to believe it was possible.

"In time they went away. I found God and He changed my life. I wanted to do His work, but I also wanted to use modern medicine to help people suffering with mental health issues. I went back to school to become a psychologist and counselor, and then I became a minister. Mi-chael, what triggered your episode today? Do you know?"

Michael shook his head. "It just came out of the blue."

"It may seem that way but there is often a trigger associated with an episode. It can be a sensation that recalls the trauma, such as pain. Strong emotions, feeling helpless, trapped or out of control can bring on a flashback or panic attack. A trigger can be as simple as a smell, a phrase, a sound."

Michael turned to look at the window. "The glass breaking. That's what triggered it today." One of the thieves had broken the glass jewelry case and triggered the alarm.

Michael gazed at Frank. "You said I can get over this."

"Recovery is a process. It takes time and there are often setbacks. It's important to stay positive, but yes, the majority of people with PTSD recover in time. For a few it is a lifelong battle. Therapy can help enormously. Talking about your trauma in a safe environment is a way to lessen the hold it has on you. How often do you have these flashbacks?"

"Three or four times a week. Sometimes every day. This is the first one since I arrived here. That was three days ago."

"And how long do they last?"

"It feels like an eternity but maybe ten minutes." Michael rubbed his thigh. It always ached worse after an episode.

Frank nodded. "And how long does it take for you to recover from one?"

"Twenty minutes or so. Will you have to tell someone about what happened today?"

"I don't but I wish you would let me help. I have a survivors' support group that meets every other week at my church. I invite you to check it out. You aren't the only one dealing with a traumatic past."

Michael shook his head. "I'd rather no one knows about this."

Especially Bethany. It shouldn't matter so much what she thought but it did matter.

Pastor Frank didn't argue. "As you wish. Please let me know if I can be of help in any way. Don't get up. I'll see myself out. I've got some plywood to cover the window. I'll be back with it in half an hour."

"I appreciate that. And for all your help earlier."

After Frank left, Michael set about building a fire in the fireplace. He was surprised that the ashes were still warm. Ivan or his friend had recently had a blaze going here. When Michael had a decent fire burning to drive off the chill, he sat down to wait for Pastor Frank's return. It wasn't long before there was a knock at the door. He got up to answer it.

Ivan stood on his doorstep looking dejected. Bethany stood behind him with her hand clamped on his shoulder.

Michael tried to disguise his rising panic. What had the boy told her?

Chapter Six

Michael didn't look happy to see her. Why should he be?

Bethany kept her chin up in spite of the mortification that weighted her down. Her brother was bent on making it harder for him to remain with her. He should be improving his behavior but he wasn't. Instead he had shown that she couldn't keep him in line. Once again she was forced to apologize for his actions.

She took a deep breath. "Good evening, Michael. I understand that Ivan broke one of the windows here. I'm truly sorry. I will have it replaced as soon as possible. In the meantime, my brother has something he wants to say to you."

"I'm sorry," Ivan mumbled.

It wasn't much of an apology, but she let it pass. "He also told me you were hurt."

"I was startled. I tripped and fell but I wasn't hurt. As you can see."

She couldn't read Michael's reaction. His face was blank. How upset was he? She wanted this awkward episode over as quickly as possible.

"I'm sure that you and I can find a way for Ivan to make amends and decide on a punishment."

"That won't be necessary."

Her brother wasn't getting off the hook so easily this time. "I insist. He needs to take responsibility for what he has done."

"I agree, but Ivan and I will work out the details. He is old enough to decide what's appropriate."

She pressed a hand to her chest. "As the adult in the family, I feel I should have a say in this." Surely he wasn't going to disregard her position as head of the family?

"Ivan and I can reach an agreement that's fair."

Her brother peered up at her. "I am old enough."

Michael nodded and stepped back. "Come in, Ivan, and we will discuss this. I'll send him home after we get the window boarded up. The pastor has gone to get some plywood."

Ivan went inside the cabin and Michael closed the door, leaving Bethany standing on the porch feeling foolish as well as incompetent.

She stomped back to the house but she couldn't stop thinking about Michael's high-handed attitude. *She* was responsible for Ivan. *She* should be a part of any discussion that involved her brother, not dismissed by some stranger as if she were a child.

Inside the house she went to the linen closet and pulled out sheets, pillows and several quilts, knowing there weren't any in the cabin. With her excuse for returning in hand, she headed out of the house. Michael Shetler had a thing or two to learn about dealing with her.

Ivan looked nervous but ready to accept his punishment. Michael walked over to the chair and sat down. The dog moved to sit beside his knee and leaned against his leg. He waited for the boy to speak first.

Ivan stuffed his hands in his pant pockets. "I'm sorry about the broken window."

"It can be fixed. What sort of punishment do you think you deserve?"

A flash of bitterness crossed Ivan's features. It was gone before Michael could be certain of what he'd seen. He leaned forward. "Why didn't Jeffrey stick around? Why didn't he stay to make sure I was okay? He has been staying here, hasn't he?"

"His dad gets mad real easy. Jeffrey sometimes hangs out here when he does. He took off tonight because he was afraid of getting in trouble at home."

Ivan took a seat beside the dog. "What happened to your leg?"

Michael wasn't prepared to have the tables turned on him but something told him that Ivan could be trusted with at least part of the truth. It might be what the boy needed to hear. "I will tell you on one condition. I don't want this mentioned to your sisters. Okay?"

The boy nodded.

"I was shot during a robbery."

"Are you joking?" Ivan's eyes grew wide.

"No joke."

"Wow. That's—I mean—you are the only person I know who has been shot."

"I would rather you didn't share the story with your sisters or your friends. It's not a pretty memory for me and I don't like pity."

"Sure. I can see you wouldn't want people talking about it. Does it still hurt?"

"All day every day but I was blessed. Other people died."

"People you knew?"

"They were my friends." Michael could feel his anxiety level rising as it did every time he thought about that night. Sadie Sue tried to climb in his lap and lick his face. He stroked her head and grew calmer.

Ivan shook his head in disbelief. "That's awful."

"The man who shot me, what kind of fellow do you think he was?"

"Evil."

"You would think so, but he wasn't much more than a scared boy pretending to be tough. Do you know what his first crime was?"

"What?"

"The first time he was arrested it was for stealing money from a neighbor. He was fourteen."

Ivan pinned his gaze to the floor. "Maybe he didn't have a choice."

Michael pushed Sadie Sue off his lap. She sat quietly beside his chair and watched him intently.

"We all have a choice. Your sister is mighty worried about you, Ivan."

The boy reached out and stroked the dog's head. "What's her name?"

Michael let him skirt around the issue of his sister's concern, knowing the boy would come back to it sooner or later. "I called her Mutt. Your sister, Jenny, named her Sadie Sue."

Ivan chuckled. "Sadie Sue. Only Jenny would think a dog needed a middle name."

"I like your little sister."

"Me, too."

"Bethany has treated me with kindness. She strikes me as a good woman."

"She treats me like I'm a little kid."

"Stop acting like one."

Ivan shot him a sour glare. "I don't. She should treat me like the man of the family."

Michael shrugged. "Being the man of the house isn't about how people treat you. The man of the family takes care of the people in his family. What have you done to take care of Bethany or Jenny lately? Think about it."

Ivan was silent for a few minutes. Finally, he looked up. "I don't have the money to pay for a new window, but I'll split wood for your fireplace for two weeks."

"A month."

"Okay, a month."

"And you are not going to skip school again, not even if Jeffrey asks you to do it."

Ivan tipped his head to the side. "How did you know Jeffrey asked me to skip with him?"

"Because Jeffrey took off tonight and left you to face the consequences alone. Something tells me he is at the bottom of some of your troubles."

Ivan scrambled to his feet. "He's my friend. You don't know anything about him."

"You're right. I don't and I'm sorry. I was wrong to say that."

Ivan relaxed his stance. "My grandfather used to say a wise man is the one who can admit when he is wrong."

"I wish I'd had the chance to meet your grandfather. I owe him a lot."

"You would have liked him."

"I'm sure of it. Ivan, you value your friend Jeffrey and rightly so, but don't value your sisters less because of that friendship. Do you understand what I'm saying?"

"I think so."

"Catch up on your schoolwork and don't skip."

"Okay."

"You should get on home now. Remember, take care of your sisters. Don't expect them to treat you like you're the man of the family. Be that man. The same way your grandfather was. They will respect you for that."

"I'll try."

Sadie Sue rushed to the door and barked once. Michael got up and went to open it, expecting Frank. Bethany stood on his doorstep, her arms loaded with linens. "I knew you would need sheets and blankets."

"Come in." He glanced at Ivan. Would the boy keep his secret? He hoped his trust wasn't misplaced. "Ivan and I have come to an agreement."

Turning to Ivan, Michael held out his hand. "We have a deal, right?"

"Right." Ivan shook on it. "I have some homework to finish. See ya." The boy went out the door, leaving Michael and Bethany alone.

* * *

Suddenly alone with Michael, Bethany stepped past him, determined to show him she wasn't intimidated by his presence. "Where would you like these?"

"On the bed will be fine."

How silly of her. Of course he would want sheets and pillows there. She crossed the room and tossed her burden on the foot of the bed. "I see you have a sleeping bag. You came prepared to rough it."

"It's not mine. I think it belongs to Ivan's friend Jeffrey. Apparently he stays here sometimes when his father is upset with him."

"I wasn't aware of that. Was that the reason the doors were locked?"

"It would be a good guess. What do you know about the boy?"

"Not much. He's been friends with Ivan since we arrived. His family lives over the ridge about a half mile as the crow flies but farther by road. His father drives a delivery truck. I don't think the mother works." She crossed her arms as she faced him. "But I'm not here to talk about Jeffrey."

"You want me to know you are in charge of Ivan, and you don't want me to interfere."

He had practically taken the words out of her

mouth. Some of her bluster ebbed away. "That's true. I'm the head of the household."

"I understand and I respect that," he said softly.

His intense gaze left her feeling exposed and vulnerable. Could he tell she doubted her ability to keep her family together? That she felt backed into a corner by the bishop's words? There was no way he could know what was in her mind yet she was sure that he did. She started for the door. "I hope you will be comfortable here."

"I hope so, too. Good night, Bethany."

The gentle way he said her name with such longing brought goose bumps to her arms. She hurried out the door before she could change her mind and stay to learn more about her unusual new neighbor.

Early the next morning the sound of someone chopping wood woke Bethany from a restless sleep. Knowing it would be useless to stay in bed, she got up and dressed for the day. Downstairs she put on a pot of coffee and enjoyed one cup in solitude. As she watched the eastern sky grow lighter, her thoughts turned to Michael. Her annoyance had vanished in the night.

Was he right to exclude her from his talk with Ivan? Last night she didn't think so, but now she was able to look at the situation without embarrassment clouding her thinking. She had been prepared to be a buffer between Ivan and Michael. She wanted her brother to make amends, but she didn't want his punishment to be unjust. Perhaps it was better that she stayed out of it and let Ivan face the consequences of his actions alone.

She glanced at the clock on the wall. Once the children were off to school she still intended to have a talk with Michael. Rising to her feet, she started on breakfast. When the eggs and oatmeal were ready, she called up the stairs. "Ivan, Jenny, time to get ready for school."

She returned to the kitchen and set plates and bowls on the table. It wasn't long before Jenny came down still in her nightgown. She made a beeline to the stove, where she warmed her hands. The upstairs bedrooms weren't heated. Hot flannel-wrapped bricks helped stave off some of the chill, but they didn't last all night. The heavy quilts only helped as long as a person stayed in bed.

When Ivan didn't appear, Bethany went to the staircase again. "Ivan. Time to get ready for school. Did you hear me?"

As she was waiting for a reply, the back door opened and he came in bundled from head to toe in his work clothes. He bent to pull off his boots. "We got four more inches of snow last night. The snowplow just went by on the road and left a huge pile of snow on our side."

She stared at him in amazement. "What were you doing outside?"

"I was chopping wood for Michael, and I shoveled the path to his house. I fed and watered our animals, too, but I didn't gather the eggs. Jenny should do that for you. I'm really hungry. What's for breakfast?"

"Scrambled eggs and oatmeal. It is nice of you to make sure Michael had wood for his fireplace."

"I have to do it for a month." He didn't sound resentful at all. He was actually smiling as he sat down at the table and pulled off his stocking cap.

"How long is he making you do my chores?" Bethany asked.

"He isn't making me do them, and they are my chores now."

Somewhat taken aback, Bethany filled their plates and took her place at the foot of the table. She looked at Ivan. "Would you like to sit at the head of the table and lead the prayers from now on?"

Both his eyebrows rose. "Really?"

It was the responsibility of the male head of an Amish household to signal the beginning and the end of the silent blessing before meals. Their grandfather had always been the one to lead prayers. After his death Bethany took over the task, never once considering that it should have fallen to Ivan. To her, he was still a child, but he wasn't little anymore.

She realized her brother was waiting for her reply. "Of course you may."

He moved his plate and sat down opposite her. Bowing his head, he clasped his hands together. Bethany did the same and silently repeated the blessing. When she was finished she waited with her head bowed for Ivan's signal. He unfolded his hands and picked up his fork. Jenny had her eyes closed. Ivan cleared his throat.

Jenny peeked at him with one eye. "Are you done?"

He nodded once. "I am."

"Goot." She reached for her glass of milk.

Ivan poured honey and milk on his oatmeal. "Jenny, I want you to gather the eggs for Bethany every day."

Jenny looked puzzled. "I do it when she asks me to."

"It will be your chore every morning before school, starting tomorrow. Bethany has enough to do."

Jenny shrugged. "Okay. Pass me a piece of toast, Ivan."

Bethany couldn't understand this sudden change in Ivan. What had Michael said to him? She wanted to ask but she didn't want to discuss it in front of her little sister. Jenny had a habit of blurting out things she had overheard.

Later, when the children were ready to go meet the bus, Bethany brought out their lunch boxes. "Ivan, did you complete the homework your teacher gave you?"

"Not all of it, but I'll stay in at recess and get the rest of it done."

"I'm pleased to hear you say that." But could she trust that he meant what he said?

"And you won't skip school again. Is that clear?" she said firmly.

"Michael and I talked about it last night. I won't skip." Ivan took his lunch box from her. "He's a *goot* fellow."

"I like him and his dog." Jenny grabbed her lunch box and headed out the door. Ivan followed close behind her, leaving Bethany more curious than ever about what Michael had said to inspire her brother.

After dressing warmly, she hiked up the hill to the cabin and knocked. She waited and knocked again but he didn't answer. She checked the barn and found his pony and cart were gone. Disappointed, she went back down the hill. Her talk with him would just have to wait.

For most of the next day and a half Michael wrestled with the notion of leaving New Covenant. He came here because he hoped the remoteness of the settlement and a change of scenery would put a stop to his anxiety attacks and flashbacks. To have such a profound episode occur within a week of his arrival was deeply disappointing. In the end he decided he had to stay. There was nowhere else to hide. He didn't want his decision to be emotional. As much as he tried to dismiss one important factor, he couldn't. Bethany was here.

If he was going to stay, he needed to work. He had a choice between building sheds with Jesse and the bishop or doing what he loved. The only drawback with repairing timepieces was that he'd be working for Bethany. He liked her. A lot. But there was no future there as long as he could fall apart at any second. His episode Sunday night had driven that fact home.

He would go back to his original plan. Bury himself in his work and remain apart from people as much as possible. He walked down the hill and found Bethany hanging wash on the line at the side of the house. Her clothesline stretched from the back porch to a nearby pine tree. A pulley system allowed her to pin her clothes on the line and move them out without stepping off the porch into the snow.

He nodded to her. "*Guder mariye*, Bethany. May I see your grandfather's workshop?"

She hesitated a fraction of a second then nodded. "Of course. It's this way."

She walked through the house into the kitchen and opened a door. "This was my grandfather's workroom."

His disappointment must have shown on his face. She tipped her head slightly. "Is something wrong?"

He didn't want a workshop attached to the house where family members could come and go as they pleased. He wanted a space all to himself. "I thought the workshop was one of the other buildings on the farm."

She shook her head. "Grandfather liked being close to us. He usually kept the door open, but if you're thinking that we will disturb you, you can keep it closed."

"I don't like interruptions while I'm working."

Her smile was forced. "That's understandable. We will make it a point to not interrupt you. You may add a bolt to the door or a lock if you prefer."

"That will not be necessary. As long as everyone's aware that I'm not to be bothered while I'm working, that should suffice." He stepped through the doorway into a tidy room with a long workbench in front of a large window. The workbench itself was made of oak. It had four shallow drawers across the front.

He opened the first drawer. Numerous screwdrivers were lined up by size in a wooden holder that had obviously been custom-made. The next drawer held a jeweler's loupe and several magnifying lenses all nestled into cotton batting. The third drawer held an assortment of gears and springs Elijah must have scavenged from clocks of all types. The fourth drawer held ledgers, receipt books, stationery and padded envelopes.

Michael looked around the room at the dozen or so clocks hanging on the walls, some in various stages of repair. The running ones ticked softly. "Your grandfather was obviously a man who took great care with his tools." He ran his finger along the top of the workbench. It was satin smooth.

"Daadi believed in a place for everything and everything in its place. He liked to use authentic old tools. He said they simply do the job better than the new ones."

"I have to agree." Along the back of the workbench were several dozen books stacked on top of each other. Michael picked up one and read the title. *"Clocks of the 1800s."*

She picked a book up and ran her fingers over the colorful cover. "Daadi would spend his free time reading about the history of clocks. I would often find him in here late at night poring over antique books on the ancient practice of clock making. I could never understand how he knew what all those little gears and wheels did."

"Repairing a clock can be complicated work, but it can also be simple when the pieces speak for themselves."

"How so?"

"Everything inside of a clock's mechanisms has a purpose. Everything is there for a reason. If you work backward, if you understand what part connects to another part and then another, the clock will tell you what each part does."

She swept her hand through the air, indicating all the timepieces on the walls. "I think you love the art of this the way he did."

"There is something fascinating and beautiful inside each clock I open. I'm happy when I can return it to someone who has treasured it. Often I see them smile when they hear a clock chime again because it brings back good memories."

She smiled softly and swiveled the old leather chair around to face her. "Good memories are important."

She looked at him. "Now that you have had a chance to see the workshop, what do you think? Are you interested in a partnership?"

"I can work in here."

She held out her hand. "Do we have a deal?"

He hesitated a second but then accepted her handshake. "We have a deal."

He held on to her fingers a few seconds longer than he needed to. She blushed as she pulled her hand away.

Bethany couldn't ignore the attraction she felt for Michael. The amazing thing was she had only known him a few days. Maybe letting him work here wasn't a good idea. For some reason she felt off balance when he looked at her with that penetrating gaze of his.

She gave herself a hard mental shake. She was being ridiculous. He needed the work and she needed the income. It wasn't like antique watch repairmen grew on trees. She would have to make sure she kept the relationship strictly business.

"Are you comfortable in the cabin?"

"It's snug. Or it will be when the new window gets in. Pastor Frank took the measurements last night. He's going to order a replacement for me."

She slipped her hands in the pockets of her apron. "Make sure the bill is sent to me. Ivan mentioned that you encouraged him to remain in school. I don't know what else you said to him but he is a changed boy. He's doing chores without being told. He's catching up on his schoolwork. Is he still splitting wood for you?"

"Without fail."

"Good. However, I still think I should have been included in the conversation."

Michael faced her. "Ivan said you treat him like a little child and not like the man of the house. I doubt he would have spoken so plainly about it if you had been in the room. I told him if he'd act like a man he would be treated as such."

"I don't agree with his assessment."

Michael grinned. "I didn't think you would. You have to admit that you don't treat him like a grown fellow."

Of all the nerve. "You haven't been around this family long enough to make an assumption like that."

"It wasn't my assumption. It was Ivan's." He smiled broadly as if inviting her to share the joke. She didn't find it funny.

"And if Ivan's change of heart wears off in a week or two, I imagine I'll be the one to blame." What possessed her to imagine she was attracted to this man? She knew from the first time they met that he was laughing at her. He was still laughing at her.

His smile faded as he seemed to realize she was upset. "I'm sure he will backslide a time or two. That's only natural. No one is looking to assign blame to you."

"That's just it. Men are assigning blame to me. The bishop, my uncle, they assume I can't control a boy Ivan's age. They want to take the problem off my hands. He isn't a problem. He's my brother. I don't know what we will do if the bishop insists on separating us, but I can tell you I won't stand still for it."

"Defying the bishop could get you shunned."

"There are other Amish communities in Maine. As much as I loved my grandfather and shared his vision for New Covenant, I will move lock, stock and barrel before I give up my brother. You don't need to worry about putting a lock on this door. I will not set foot in this room while you are here."

She walked out and slammed the door behind her.

Chapter Seven

"You should invite Michael to eat with us," Ivan said at the dinner table three days after Michael had moved into the cabin.

Bethany had spent much of the time regretting her outburst. She owed him an apology. Michael wasn't the cause of her problem. She shouldn't have taken her ill temper out on him. He had been trying to help.

Michael *had* helped although the bishop might not be able to see the improvement in Ivan's attitude. She was also certain he wouldn't simply take her word for it.

"Why can't Sadie Sue eat with us, too?" Jenny asked.

Bethany leveled a don't-be-ridiculous look at Jenny. "Because I won't allow a dog in the house at mealtime. I don't care how much you like her. As for Michael, I haven't asked him because he specifically said that he likes working alone and he likes his privacy. Now that he is going to be working in Grandfather's shop, I want you both to understand that when that door is closed you are not to go in there."

"But what if I need something?" Jenny asked.

Bethany put down her fork to stare at her sister. "What could you possibly need from Grandfather's workshop?"

"I don't know. I might need to play with Sadie Sue. She likes to fetch sticks."

Bethany tried not to smile at her sister's cajoling tone. "I'm sure there will be plenty of times that you can play with her. Just not while Michael is working."

Ivan helped himself to another dollop of potatoes. "Michael might like to work alone but that doesn't mean he likes to eat alone. You should ask him."

"I'll consider it." That was all she was going to say on the subject. "Are you excited about having Thanksgiving dinner tomorrow at the Lapp farm?"

Jenny held her hand high in the air. "I am. No school for four days."

Bethany looked at her brother. "What about you, Ivan?"

"Jeffrey won't be there. I won't have anyone to hang out with."

"I'm sure that the Miller boys will include you in any games they start." The trio of cousins were in their late teens but they normally included Ivan in their group sports during church get-togethers. There were so few people in New Covenant yet. She wasn't sure that all of those would stay after enduring a Maine winter.

"Is Michael going to be there?" Ivan looked at her hopefully.

Bethany thought back over the times she and Michael had spent together. "I don't believe I mentioned it to him. Jesse may have told him about it."

Ivan pushed back his chair. "I'll go invite him."

"After you finish your supper." Although Bethany hadn't liked hearing that she treated Ivan as a child, she had to admit there were some things their grandfather had done that Ivan could take over.

"I thought perhaps you could read some passages from the Bible for us tonight. I have to work on Jenny's Christmas program costume."

"You really want me to?" He looked amazed.

"Absolutely."

"Sure. I'd be happy to do that. When I'm finished eating can I invite Michael to the Thanksgiving dinner?"

She glanced at the door and then back to her brother. "You'll have to go outside and check if there is a light in the workshop windows. If there is, wait until he is finished working. If there isn't a light, go ahead and go up to the cabin. But first, how was your day at school?"

"I'm caught up on my work." His comment lacked enthusiasm. He wouldn't meet her gaze.

"I'm happy to hear that. What else happened today?"

"Somebody said I stole money from their locker. I didn't but I'm not sure the teacher believed me. She looked through my desk and didn't find anything."

"Oh, Ivan, I'm sorry."

"It's okay."

It wasn't okay but Bethany didn't know how to deal with it. Her brother had built himself a bad reputation. Repairing it would take time. Time he might not have. The bishop would be at the dinner tomorrow. Could she convince him that Ivan had seen the error of his ways after the bishop had heard Jedidiah's tale?

Michael's input might sway the bishop if he could be convinced to attend the dinner. He knew Ivan was chopping wood each day and doing his chores and doing better in school.

She pushed the chicken casserole around on her plate as her appetite vanished. The bishop wouldn't hear Michael's observations if Michael didn't speak to him. She was going to have to apologize to Michael and then ask him to speak on Ivan's behalf as a favor.

Her chicken casserole might as well have been crow. That was what was on the menu for later.

"Ivan, I'll invite Michael to the Thanksgiving dinner at the Lapps' tomorrow. I want you to help your sister practice her lines for the Christmas program."

He looked ready to object but nodded instead. "Okay. I will."

She rose from her chair. "*Danki.* The two of you clear the table. I'm going to speak with Michael."

"Invite Sadie Sue, too," Jenny said.

"*Nee*, I will not invite the dog. If you wish to do something special for her you will have to do it here."

"Can I bake her some cookies?"

"Learn your lines for the Christmas program first."

"All right," Jenny said, but she didn't look happy about it.

Bethany checked the workshop first. The light was off. He must've gone home. She trudged up the hill, bemoaning how quickly it got dark this time of year. As she drew near the cabin she saw Michael was filling a pair of pails at the pump in the yard. His dog sat by his side. She woofed several times, causing him to look around. He caught sight of Bethany and stopped. He watched her with a hint of uncertainty in his eyes. She couldn't blame him.

She forged ahead. "It seems like I am apologizing every time I see you."

He just stared at her.

He wasn't making it easy.

"I wanted to say that I'm sorry for the way I behaved the other day. Although it isn't really an excuse, I am very concerned about my brother. I do not want to send him to live with our uncle. Onkel Harvey is a good man, don't get me wrong. He has a fine family. My reason for wanting to keep Ivan with me is a selfish one. I love my brother. I promised my mother as she lay dying that I would take care of Ivan and Jenny. I don't want to break that promise."

"That's understandable. You are forgiven. There was no need for you to come and apologize."

She pressed a hand to her chest. "I *needed* to apologize."

He picked up one bucket of water and started toward the barn. Bethany picked up the second bucket and followed him. He frowned as he glanced at her. "I can manage this."

"Many hands make light work. Did you find everything you need in my grandfather's workshop today?"

"I did, plus I have many of my own tools."

"I guess that makes sense." In the barn she put the bucket down as he poured the first one into a small tank in the pony's stall. He handed her the empty pail, picked up the full one and poured it into the tank, as well.

He walked out of the barn and Bethany followed him. It appeared that he wasn't in the mood to talk. She followed him anyway.

"I don't know if Jesse mentioned it but our church community is having a Thanksgiving dinner tomorrow. I wanted to make sure you knew you were invited."

"I'll be working."

"It will be a great opportunity to get to know the other Amish families here."

"I'll meet them in time."

"Why wait?" She tried to sound cheerful not desperate.

"Because I'm working tomorrow."

She had hoped she wouldn't have to beg but he left her no choice. "All right, I have a favor to ask of you."

A slight smile curved his lips. "Really? I can't wait to hear this. Has Clarabelle given you the name of a new marriage prospect that you want me to check out?"

"I wish you would forget about the cow."

"I've tried but I can't. It's stuck in my brain."

"Oh, never mind." She turned to go. She'd only taken a few steps when he spoke again.

"Wait. What is it that you need?"

She stayed where she was with her hands pushed deep into the pockets of her coat, so he couldn't see how tightly clenched her fingers were. "The bishop will be there. I need your help convincing him that Ivan has had a change of heart. That he's doing better." She stared at the ground, afraid to see him refuse. "Will you do that? Please?"

Michael groaned inwardly. She had no idea what she was asking. A dinner with dozens of strangers in an unfamiliar house. A crowd. The noise. He grew tense just thinking about it.

Why did she have to look so dejected? So vulnerable? Why was she pinning her hopes on him? It would be amazing if he didn't end the dinner as a babbling ball of fear hiding under the table. He couldn't do it.

She glanced at him from beneath lowered lashes.

How could he not do it?

She wanted to keep her family together. He prayed for strength for the first time in months. Sadie Sue whined as she gazed up at him. "I know, I know. It's a bad idea."

He crossed the few steps between them and

stopped inches from Bethany. He lifted her chin so she would look at him. "Okay, I'll do it, but you must understand that my words may not carry much weight. I'm new here. I'm not even a member of your congregation yet."

He would speak to the man and then leave. He didn't have to stay for the meal. He would come home and work in peace.

The joy on Bethany's face was almost worth the discomfort he knew he was going to endure. Beneath his fingers her skin was soft as the silk cloths he used to polish his work. Her beautiful eyes were damp with unshed tears. Her lips were red because she had been biting them. He wanted to soothe them with a kiss.

As sure as the sun would rise again tomorrow, he knew one kiss would not be enough.

He stepped away from her. She blinked rapidly and swiped at her unshed tears with both hands. *"Danki."*

"Please tell me I don't have to cook something and take it to eat."

Her laugh was shaky. "I'll make enough for both of us."

"Where is this party taking place?"

"At the Lapp farm. It's about a half mile from here. You met Gemma the other night. The farm belongs to her parents. We might as well ride together, don't you think? I have to take some tables and chairs for them to use. I'll pick you up at noon. That should give you plenty of time to meet people before they start serving at two o'clock."

A half mile wasn't too far. He could walk that distance home alone.

Bethany grabbed his hand. "Bless you. I mean that from the bottom of my heart. Bless you and the good you are doing for my family."

"I'm doing it for Ivan. The kid deserves a break."

She let go of him and pushed her hands deep into her coat pockets. "Of course. He may not realize it yet, but you are a true friend."

As she hurried away he shook his head. Thanksgiving Day would end in disaster for him. He looked down at Sadie Sue. "I am an idiot. Did you know that? You've adopted an idiot for a master."

Michael waited on the porch with his back against the side of the cabin as Bethany drove up in a large wagon the next morning. The children were sitting beside her. His nerves had been on edge since he woke well before dawn. Sadie Sue was shut inside the cabin. He wished he could take her with him.

"Happy Thanksgiving," Bethany called out. The children echoed her greeting. They were staring at him.

All he had to do was walk down the steps and get in her wagon. His palms were damp; his heart was racing. He counted to three and pushed away from the wall. Bethany had Ivan and Jenny get in the back, giving him more room. Getting up onto the seat was easier said than done. The wagon seat was much higher than a buggy. It wasn't graceful but he finally hauled himself up and onto the padded wooden bench.

"All set," he muttered between his clenched teeth.

"Thank you again for doing this."

"Sure, no problem." He hoped.

"I don't see Sadie," Jenny said.

"I locked her in the house." He couldn't believe how much he'd come to rely on the dog. She alerted him when someone was near. When she was at ease, he was at ease.

Bethany spoke to the team and the wagon lurched forward, jarring his leg. Out on the roadway the going was smoother. He let go of his death grip on the side of the seat.

Bethany glanced his way. "Is your leg paining you?"

"Some. I think there's a change in weather coming."

"The newspaper this morning said we could expect a significant snowstorm over the next three days."

"What is 'significant' to the people of Maine?"

"Two, maybe three, in places."

"Inches?"

"Feet," she said with a smile. "Don't worry. Jesse plows our lanes open with his big team but you should invest in some snowshoes before long."

Snowshoes and a cane. How was that going to work? Maybe moving here had been a mistake.

It didn't take long to reach the Lapp farm. Bethany drew the horse to a stop by the front door. The children jumped off the back of the wagon and ran inside. Bethany turned to him. "Can I help you get down?"

He shook his head. "I don't need help. Besides, if I fall I only want one person to get hurt."

She ignored him, jumped down and came around to his side. "I won't let you fall."

"I should believe a woman who talks to cows? Stand aside." He grimaced as he swung his bad leg over the side.

"Nope. Keep one hand on the seat and put your other hand on my shoulder and lower your weight slowly."

"I'm not getting down until you're out of the way."

"You will get very cold sitting here when the sun goes down."

"Stubborn woman."

"I've been called that before."

"Why am I not surprised." He searched for a way to get down without help. It was a long drop. "Okay, I hate to admit it, but your idea looks like my best option."

He gave her his cane and she leaned it against the wagon wheel. Placing his hand on her shoulder, he scooted over the edge of the seat and started to lower himself to the ground.

One horse took a step forward. The cane fell, clattering against the wheel spokes. The other horse tossed her head and took a step, jerking the wagon. Michael lost his grip on the seat and pulled Bethany off balance.

The second he started to fall Bethany wrapped her arms around him and threw herself over backward, trying to take the brunt of his weight. Her head struck the ground with a painful-sounding thump. She didn't make a sound.

"Are you okay? Bethany, are you okay? Speak to me." Michael was holding himself above her on his forearms. His face was inches from hers. Her lids fluttered up. She looked at him and blinked twice.

"You have pretty eyes." Her voice was a bare whisper.

"What?"

She closed her eyes. "Nothing. I'm okay. Are you hurt?"

At least she was talking. "My pride has a big dent in it, but I don't think anything is broken."

"Then could you get off me? You're very heavy." She winced in pain.

"What is going on here?"

Michael looked up to see an older Amish man with a graying beard glaring at him. Jesse stood at his side.

"Hi, Jesse." Michael rolled off Bethany and lay sprawled beside her. His bad leg was on fire, his shoulders ached, and he had skinned both hands trying to keep his full weight from crashing down on her.

"Michael?" Jesse's eyebrows rose until they touched the brim of his black hat.

"It's me. Happy Thanksgiving."

"What are you doing on the ground?"

Michael laughed even though it hurt. "I put my trust in a woman who has conversations with her cow. Big mistake." He turned his head to gaze at Bethany. "Are you sure you aren't hurt?"

"I'm still checking." She pressed a hand to the back of her head.

Her friend Gemma came out of the house. "What has happened? Bethany, is that you?"

Bethany pushed herself into a sitting position. "Hello, Gemma. Happy Thanksgiving."

Jesse was still frowning at Michael. "I don't understand what you are doing on the ground."

"Bethany kindly gave me a ride here, and when I was trying to get out of her wagon, I fell on her. It was an accident. I think she hit her head pretty hard."

Gemma helped Bethany to her feet. "You poor thing. Are you injured?"

Bethany managed a half-hearted smile. "Only bumps and bruises. I'm afraid Michael is the one who is hurt."

Michael struggled to his feet with Jesse's assistance and leaned against the wagon. "I'm fine. Where's my cane?"

The elderly Amish man beside Jesse picked it up and handed it to Michael with a scowl on his face. "I am Bishop Schultz."

"Just the man I wanted to see. I'm Michael Shetler. I'm a newcomer to the area."

The bishop stroked his beard as he stared at Michael. "Jesse has told me about you."

"I need to unpack the tables and chairs," Bethany said.

"Someone else can take care of that. You need a few minutes' rest to regain your wits," Michael told her in a stern tone.

She scowled at him. "My wits are not scattered."

"That's open to debate. You hit your head pretty hard. You could have a concussion. Gemma, make her go inside and rest."

Michael caught the sidelong glare Bethany shot at him. She wasn't happy to have him telling her what to do. Too bad. In his opinion, she was too pale. He didn't want her keeling over and spoiling the party. That was his job.

Gemma smiled kindly at Michael as she took Bethany's arm. "He is right. Come in. I have some fresh brewed sweet tea and my special lemon cookies, and I'm going to fix an ice pack for your head."

"I would speak with you, Bethany, when you are recovered," Bishop Schultz said. Bethany grew a shade paler.

Inside the house the mouthwatering smells of roasting turkey, fresh baked breads and pumpkin pies filled the air. Michael saw Ivan seated beside two teenage boys looking through a hunting magazine. He beckoned to the boy. "Ivan, can I see you a minute?"

Ivan came over. "What's up?"

"Ask your friends to help you bring in the tables and chairs from the back of the wagon and take care of the horses."

"Sure." He went back to the boys and they all walked outside. A few minutes later they came in carrying the extra seating. Gemma's mother directed them where to set up. Another family arrived with baskets of food, and a festive air began to fill the room as happy chatter and laughter grew in volume.

Michael stayed beside Bethany, who was seated in a wingback chair near the fireplace. She soon had a plate of cookies on her lap and a glass of tea in her hand. Her color was already better when Gemma brought her the ice pack. Michael knew Bethany had taken the brunt of the fall trying to protect him. It should have been the other way around.

His gaze was constantly drawn to her. Her color returned to normal, but the longer he watched her the more flushed she became. Every time he caught her eye she looked away.

After ten minutes, Bethany set her empty glass aside. "I should be helping in the kitchen."

Bethany couldn't take Michael staring at her another minute. Didn't he realize everyone was noticing his attention? She blushed at being the recipient of so many speculative looks. She was about to get up when the bishop approached her with Jedidiah a few steps behind him.

The bishop settled himself in a nearby chair. "Are you feeling recovered, Bethany?"

"I have a headache that I'm sure will get better quickly. Jedidiah, did you get my letter and the check?"

"I did. It was a fair price, though the cost was not the issue. I trust Ivan will repay you?"

She clasped her hands together. "I want you both to know that my brother has improved his attitude one hundred percent since that incident."

"Even if that is true, it is too little too late." The bishop's stern look chilled her.

She gestured to Michael. "This is Michael Shetler. He has taken over Grandfather's watch repair business. He can attest to Ivan's improvements. He has seen it firsthand."

"In what way?" Jedidiah asked.

"The boy broke a window in the cabin I rented from Bethany. I had a talk with him. We settled on his punishment. He has split wood for me every morning, has taken over many of Bethany's outdoor chores, and he has improved his grades at school. I believe his friend has been the instigator of much of the trouble Ivan has been in."

The bishop folded his arms over his chest. "If that is true, the boy has shown bad judgment in his choice of friends."

Jedidiah shifted his weight from one foot to the other. "I spoke with his teacher yesterday evening. We happened to be in the grocery store at the same time. She tells me some of the *Englisch* children have accused Ivan of stealing money."

"One child did. She searched his desk and didn't find anything. It wasn't Ivan," Bethany insisted.

The bishop's face grew somber. "I wish I could give him the benefit of the doubt, but there have been too many instances where he has been involved. Jedidiah has offered to take the boy until his uncle arrives. He feels he can give Ivan the supervision he needs. I have agreed to this."

"*Nee*, you can't take him from me. You can't."

"What if I were to take responsibility for the boy?" Michael offered.

Chapter Eight

Michael was certain that he had lost his mind. The look on Bethany's face told him she thought he was her hero.

The bishop regarded him intently. "Are you sure you understand what this means?"

"I do. I will oversee the boy's discipline. I will stand as substitute for his father. Any person who has difficulties or accusations against the boy can address them with me. If you will allow me, then the boy does not have to leave Bethany's care or his home. Should he go to live with Jedidiah now, he will be unable to complete the bargain he has with me."

The bishop nodded slowly. "I appreciate what Jedidiah has offered. I didn't feel right taking the boy from his sister's care, but I saw no other choice after Jedidiah told me about the theft of his goods. You have given me one. You are new to us but Jesse has vouched for your character, Michael, otherwise I would not agree to this, but I trust his judgment. This arrangement will be only until the boy's uncle arrives at Christmas," the bishop added. "I want to be clear that this isn't a permanent situation, and that you are accepting financial responsibility as well as a moral responsibility to see that Ivan behaves himself."

"I understand that."

Bethany's hopeful gaze was pinned on Michael. "You don't have to do this."

He considered retracting his offer but he wasn't prepared to see the Martin family split up. "I understand that. I want to do it. I'll speak to Ivan about it when we get home today."

"Agreed." The bishop smiled broadly. Even Jedidiah looked relieved. The two men walked away.

"I can't thank you enough," Bethany said with tears in her eyes.

"Let's hope Ivan feels the same way." He was already regretting his rash gesture. His intention was to spend less time with Bethany and her family, not more.

Bethany heard the hesitancy in Michael's voice. "You won't be sorry you did this. It proves that you believe in my brother and that is priceless to me."

Michael rubbed his hands on his pants. "I think I need some fresh air."

He left the room. Once he was out of sight, Gemma hurried over to sit beside Bethany. "What was that all about?"

"Ivan."

"I was afraid that's what the bishop had on his mind when he cornered you. Is he still sending the boy away at Christmas?"

"He wanted to send him to live with Jedidiah until then, but Michael volunteered to be responsible for him."

"How did you manage that?"

"It was his own idea."

Gemma leaned forward eagerly. "Tell me all about your mystery man."

"There isn't much to tell. Apparently, he corresponded with Daadi about working for him. He had already paid the first and last months' rent on the cabin. He likes to keep to himself. And he's from Sugarcreek, Ohio."

"I don't mean the dry details. Does he have a girlfriend back in Ohio? Is he looking to marry? Does he have money?"

"How would I know that?"

Gemma chuckled. "You don't know how to snoop. I could find all that out in ten minutes."

"I'm not so sure. He doesn't like to talk about himself."

"Then he is hiding something. I wonder what it is. How did he know your grandfather?"

"He didn't really. A jeweler by the name of George Meyers recommended Michael to my grandfather and that's all I know. He and Ivan get along. I'm grateful for that."

"You like him, don't you?"

Bethany was wary of the eager look in her friend's eyes. "He's nice enough."

"I'd say he's a lot better than Jesse Crump or Jedidiah. I can't believe he fell into your lap and all you can say is that he's nice enough. He is the answer to your prayers."

"What are you talking about?"

"You need a husband by Christmas and Michael Shetler appears out of the blue. God moves in mysterious ways."

"You're being ridiculous. There is nothing between us."

"I wouldn't say that. I noticed the way he looked at you when he was sitting beside you. We all noticed. He's interested. The man has potential. With a little effort on your part, you could have him eating out of your hand. I've got to go help Mamm. Can I get you anything else?"

Bethany shook her head and winced. She pressed a hand to the back of her aching head. "I'm gonna sit here with my ice pack for a little longer."

Gemma patted Bethany's knee. "Let me know if you need anything."

Jenny came running to Bethany's side along with Sadie Sue. "Look, sister. I didn't invite her. She came all by herself."

"I wonder how she got out." Bethany stared at the dog. She was sure Michael had locked her in.

Sadie's attention turned to the tables where the food was being set out. She licked her chops. Bethany foresaw a disaster. "*Nee*, Jenny, take her outside."

"But why?"

"Because I asked you to."

"Okay. Come on, Sadie Sue." Jenny headed toward the back door, taking Sadie within a few feet of the table and a steaming plate of sausages. The dog stopped and eyed the dish as Jenny went out the door. No one else was near the dog.

Bethany rose from her chair. "*Nee*, Sadie Sue. Don't do it."

Jenny opened the back door and looked in. "Sadie, come on."

The dog gave the sausages a forlorn glance and trotted out the door. Bethany sank back in her chair with a sigh of relief.

"Was that my dog?" Michael asked as he came in from outside.

"*Ja*, it was Sadie Sue." Remembering Gemma's comments, Bethany found herself tongue-tied. Did he find her attractive? Or was his attentiveness just part of his makeup that had nothing to do with her? Bethany wished she could tell what he was thinking.

He scratched the back of his head. "I wonder how she got out of the house."

Bethany shrugged.

"How are you feeling?" he asked.

"Better." She kept her demeanor cool. Were people watching them and speculating? She caught sight of Gemma smiling widely. Her friend winked.

"I'm glad to hear you are better. I'm going to go take Sadie home and see how she escaped. I hope we don't have to replace another windowpane."

"Will you be coming back?"

"*Nee*, you stay and enjoy your friends. I have work to do."

She didn't want him to go. She was torn by her conflicting feelings. "Don't you even want something to eat?"

"I have plenty back at the cabin. Get someone to drive you home if you aren't feeling better."

"Ivan can drive the wagon."

Michael nodded and walked away. When he opened the door he glanced back at her with such a look of longing that it startled her. Was there something between them and she had been too blind to see it?

Bethany decided the family would walk to the church service on Sunday instead of taking the

buggy. The preaching was being held at the home
of Nigel and Becca Miller. Their farm was little
more than a quarter of a mile beyond the Lapp
place. Nigel was a carpenter who made furniture
in the off-season.

An unexpectedly warm southern wind was
melting the snow, making the sunshine feel
even brighter. Rivulets of water trickled along
the ditches and flowed out of the snow-covered
fields. Amish families—some on foot, most in
buggies—were all headed in the same direction.
Cheerful greetings and pleasant exchanges filled
the crisp air. Everyone was glad to see a break
in the weather.

Bethany declined numerous offers of a ride,
content to stretch her legs on such a fine morning. The icy grip of winter would return all too
soon. Jenny and Ivan trudged along beside her,
enjoying the sunshine.

She turned in at the farm lane where a dozen
buggies were lined up on the hillside just south
of the barn. The horses, still wearing their har-
nesses, were tied up along a split-rail fence, content to munch on the hay spread in front of them
or doze in the sunshine.

The early morning activity was focused around
the barn. Men were busy unloading backless seats
from the large gray boxlike bench wagon that
was used to transport the benches from home to

home for the services held every other Sunday. Bishop Schultz was supervising the unloading. When the wagon was empty, he conferred with his minister.

Bethany entered the house. Inside, it was a flurry of activity as the women arranged food on counters and tables. Several small children were being watched over by the Millers' niece. She beckoned Jenny to come help her. The Miller boys were outside playing a game of tag and Ivan went to join them.

Catching sight of Gemma unpacking baskets of food, Bethany crossed the room toward them and handed over her basket of food for the lunch that would be served after the service. "*Guder mariye*, Gemma."

"Good morning, Bethany. Isn't the weather wonderful?"

"It is." Turning to Becca Miller, Bethany grinned at the baby she held. Little Daniel was six months old with a wide toothless grin and a head of white-blond curls. "Wow, how this little boy is growing. May I hold him?"

"Of course. I hate to admit it but he gets heavy quickly these days." Becca handed the baby over with a timid smile.

Bethany took Daniel and held him to her shoulder, enjoying the feel of a baby in her arms and his wonderful smell. "You're not so heavy."

"He should be. He eats like a little piglet." There was nothing but love in Becca's eyes as she gazed at her son.

Gemma said, "I see the bishop and minister coming. We'd best hurry and join the others in the barn."

As she spoke, Bishop Schultz and Samuel Yoder entered the house and went upstairs, where they would discuss the preaching that was to be done that morning. The three-to-four-hours-long service would be preached without the use of notes. Each man had to speak as God moved him.

Bethany handed the baby back to Becca. The women quickly finished their tasks and left the house.

The barn was already filled with people sitting quietly on rows of backless wooden benches with the women on one side of the aisle and men on the other side. Tarps had been hung over ropes stretched between upright timbers to cordon off an area for the service. Behind them, the sounds of cattle, horses and pigs could be heard. The south-facing doors were open to catch what warmth the sunshine and wind could provide.

Bethany took her place among the unmarried women. Gemma and Jenny sat beside her. In front of them sat the married women, several holding infants. Becca slipped a string of beads and buttons from her pocket. She handed them to her little one. He was then content and played quietly with his toy. Her older boys sat beside their father.

From the men's side of the aisle, the song leader announced the hymn. There was a wave of rustling and activity as people opened their thick black songbooks. The *Ausbund* contained the words of all the hymns but no musical scores. The songs, sung from memory, had been passed down through countless generations. They were sung slowly and in unison by people opening their hearts to receive God's presence without the distraction of musical instruments. The slow cadence allowed everyone to focus on the meaning of each word.

At the end of the first hymn, Bethany took a moment to glance toward the men's side. She spotted Michael sitting behind the married men with Ivan. Her brother squirmed in his seat, looking restless. Michael, on the other hand, held his songbook with a look of intense devotion on his face.

He glanced in her direction and she smiled at him. He immediately looked away and she felt the pinch of his rejection. She hadn't spoken to him since Thanksgiving. Was something wrong? Was he regretting his decision to mentor Ivan? Her brother was thrilled. He didn't object to Michael standing in his father's role.

The song leader announced the second hymn,

"O Gott Vater, wir Loben dich" ("Oh God the Father, We Praise You"). It was always the second hymn of an Amish service. Bethany forgot about Michael and her brother as she joined the entire congregation in singing God's praise, asking that the people present would receive His words and take them into their hearts.

At the end of the second hymn, the minister and Bishop Schultz came in and hung their hats on pegs set in the wall. That was the signal that the preaching would now begin. Bethany tried to listen closely to what was being said, but she found her mind wandering to the subject of Michael. What might he be looking for in a wife?

Michael sat up straight and unobtrusively stretched his bad leg. He was still stiff after his fall on Thursday. The wooden benches were not made for comfort. At least he hadn't fallen asleep the way their host Nigel Miller was doing. A few minutes after the preaching started, the farmer started nodding off in front of Michael. When Nigel began to tip sideways, Michael reached up and caught his arm before he tumbled off his seat.

Nigel jerked awake. *"Danki,"* he whispered as he gave Michael a sheepish grin.

Michael ventured a guess. "Working late?"

Nigel shook his head. "Colicky baby."

He leaned forward to look over at the women.

Following his gaze, Michael saw Nigel's wife sitting across the aisle. Becca Miller held the baby sleeping sweetly in her arms. Her face held an expression of pure happiness when she caught her husband's glance. Bethany sat behind her.

What Michael wouldn't give to see Bethany look at him with a similar light in her eyes.

He quickly focused on his hymnal. Such daydreaming was foolishness. He wasn't husband material. He might never be. He tried to push thoughts of Bethany aside but they came back to him at odd times and more often than he cared to admit. He hadn't had another flashback or panic episode since the previous Sunday, but that didn't mean he was well.

Three hours into the service, the bishop stopped speaking and the song leader called out the number of the final hymn. Michael ventured a look in Bethany's direction. She held her songbook open for Jenny seated beside her. She pointed out the words as she sang them.

Bethany should have children of her own. She would make a good mother. He couldn't imagine why God had chosen not to bless her with a husband and children of her own. It didn't seem right.

The song drew to a close. Ivan was up and out the doors the second it ended. Teenage boys were expected to sit at the very back. Michael always assumed it was so their late arrivals and quick getaways didn't disrupt others. He followed more slowly. His eyes were drawn to Bethany as she walked toward the farmhouse with the other women.

How much of his life would he spend like this, watching her from afar, wishing for something that could never happen? Months? Years? What if he never got well?

On Monday afternoon just before the children came home from school, Bethany got out her crafting supplies and spread them on the table. She made a batch of oatmeal cookies and a pot of peppermint hot chocolate and left it simmering on the back of the stove.

She was cutting and folding card stock paper when Ivan and Jenny came in the door. Jenny's eyes lit up. "Is it time to make our Christmas cards?"

"*Ja*, it is time. Do you have your lists of the people you want to send them to?"

Both children were well prepared and provided a list of more than a dozen people each that they would handcraft a greeting card for. Bethany had her own list that included every family in the New Covenant congregation as well as Pastor Frank, the children's teachers, bus driver and many of the merchants in town that she did business with.

After two mugs each of the hot chocolate and a plate of cookies, they were laughing and sharing ideas for cards. Jenny loved to draw a snow-covered tree branch with a cardinal sitting on it. She added silver glitter to the snow and red glitter to the birds. Ivan liked making construction paper cutouts of a horse and sleigh and gluing them to the card stock. He covered the snowy foreground with glitter. Bethany enjoyed making snowmen out of cotton balls glued together inside the card.

Before long there was glitter on the table, glitter on the floor and glitter on the children, but Bethany didn't care. She had to make this Christmas a special one in case they weren't together next year. "Ivan, you didn't tell me what song you'll be singing at the community Christmas program." Since religious-themed programs could no longer be held in the public schools, the community had decided to keep the Christmas pageant alive and well in the community center. The children and their teachers who wished to participate were eagerly welcomed.

Ivan didn't look up from crafting his card. "I'm going to sing 'O Come, O Come, Emmanuel.'"

"That's one of my favorites. Will you sing it for me now?" she asked with a catch in her throat.

He did and there were tears in her eyes by the time he finished. "That was fine. God has blessed you with a wonderful singing voice."

Jenny laid down her scissors. "I want to sing a song."

Bethany blinked away her tears and smiled. "What song would you like to perform?"

"'Go Tell It on the Mountain.'"

"That's a fine song. Let's all sing it together." Bethany hummed the first note and they all joined in singing at the top of their lungs to the very last verse.

"I don't know how you expect me to get any work done with all the noise and the delicious smell of hot chocolate coming from this room."

Bethany looked up to see Michael standing in the doorway with an indulgent smile lighting his face. Sadie Sue ambled over to Jenny. She got a hug and a pat before settling to the floor beside Jenny's chair with a sprinkling of red glitter across her head.

Bethany pointed at Michael. "That door is to remain closed while you are working."

He held his hands wide. "I'm done for the evening."

"In that case, pull up a chair and start making your Christmas cards. They have to go in the mail by the end of this week if you want them to arrive on time."

"I haven't sent many cards in the last few years, but I will definitely take some of that hot chocolate. Is that peppermint I smell?"

"Help yourself. I will make a list of people for you. Let's start with your mother and father. They will get a card, right?"

He nodded as he filled a white mug from the pot. "I have three brothers and two sisters."

She wrote down the names and addresses that he gave her. She sat poised with a pen. "Grandparents?"

"Gone, I'm afraid."

"Mr. Meyers at the jewelry store where you used to work? Grandfather always sent him one. How about some of the people you worked with? Are you still friends with them?"

He paused with the mug halfway to his mouth. He slowly lowered it. "I don't have friends there anymore."

He put the mug down, walked back into the workroom and closed the door.

Bethany didn't know what to make of his abrupt retreat. She looked at Ivan. "Did I say something wrong?"

Ivan shrugged. "He was shot during a robbery there. He doesn't like to talk about it."

Bethany stared at her brother, unsure she'd heard him correctly. "Michael was shot?"

Ivan nodded. "That's why he limps. I wasn't supposed to tell you. You won't tell him I mentioned it, will you?"

Bethany shook her head. "I won't say anything."

No wonder Michael didn't like to talk about his injury. Someone had robbed him at gunpoint and shot him. Was he the only one? Or were there others, too? She thought back to something her grandfather had mentioned. He told her the man who sent him watches to fix had a store robbed. Somewhere she had her grandfather's correspondences. He kept everything in case he had to prove the work had been done and the timepieces had been returned.

Some things about Michael began to make sense. The way he was always vigilant. He didn't like crowds. He often stood with his back to the wall. She assumed he was leaning against the wall to rest his leg, but he might just as easily have been doing it to assure himself there was no one behind him.

She looked at Ivan and Jenny. "Let's make Christmas cards for Michael's family. It can be our Christmas gift to him. What do you think?" They both agreed and got to work.

Later that evening, Bethany carried a lantern into her grandfather's room. She put it down on his bedside table and pulled a large box from under his bed. She opened it and began to search for letters from George Meyers. She found the one she was looking for. Holding it in her hand, Bethany was torn by the feeling that she was invading Michael's privacy by snooping into his past. Would it tell her what she needed to know about Michael and what troubled him? Like her brother, she didn't know how to help Michael if she didn't know what was wrong.

She opened the letter and began reading.

Chapter Nine

Michael peered through his jeweler's loupe at a tiny screw he was attempting to insert into the mechanism of an antique gold pocket watch. His concentration was broken by the thump-thump-thump of Sadie Sue's tail against the floor. It was her signal that he wasn't alone but the visitor was someone she knew.

He couldn't believe what a difference having the dog had made on his anxiety level. He was confident in her ability to alert him to strangers. He didn't feel the need to constantly scan his surroundings for danger as often. When he did get agitated, she would distract him by nuzzling him for affection or bringing him the red ball she loved to fetch and dropping it in his lap.

"What are you doing?" Jenny asked as she came up beside him. His workbench was just high enough to allow her to rest her hands and chin on it.

"I'm working. Are you supposed to be in here?"

"I can't come in when the door is closed."

"Is the door closed, Jenny?" He turned the loupe up so that he could see her face. She was the perfect picture of boredom.

"It was closed but then it opened, so I came in."

He tipped his head to the side. "Did it open because you turned the doorknob?"

"Maybe. Are you mad?"

He sighed heavily. "What do you need, Jenny?"

"I want someone to play hide-and-seek with me. Will you, please?"

"I'm working. Ask your sister to play with you."

"She's doing the laundry."

"Then perhaps your brother would enjoy playing with you."

"He says I'm too little and that I'm just a pest. I'm not a pest, am I?"

Michael put down his screwdriver. The tiny screw popped off the magnetized end and went rolling off the workbench onto the floor. He pressed his lips into a hard line. "You are not a pest, but I don't have time to play, Jenny. I have work to do."

Her hopeful expression dissolved into a serious pout.

He got off his stool and awkwardly dropped to one knee to see under the bench. Jenny picked the screw up and handed it to him. "No one wants to play with me."

He paused and thought for a minute. "Why aren't you in school?"

"'Cause the teachers have to go to meetings for two days."

He got back on his work stool. "Play with Sadie."

"Sadie Sue can't play hide-and-seek. She can't count."

He put his loupe back on. "I'm sure Sadie can learn to play hide-and-seek with a little help from you. You go hide, and I will send her to find you." If he was fortunate, he could have ten or twenty minutes of uninterrupted work time before she came looking for the dog.

Bethany opened the door. "Jenny, I thought I told you to stay out of the workroom while Michael is in here."

"He wants me to play with Sadie Sue."

Bethany folded her arms across her chest. "Then bring the dog with you and leave Michael alone."

"We're playing hide-and-seek. I'm going to go hide. Michael, you count for her." Jenny took off at a run.

He waited a long moment, then looked at his dog. "Ten." She wagged her tail.

Bethany grinned at him. She had the most contagious smile. It boosted his spirits every time he saw it. "I'm sorry Jenny bothered you. She has been out of school for the past two days because of teachers' meetings. I think she has a touch of cabin fever."

"I'm ready," Jenny called from somewhere in the house.

Michael looked down at the dog. "Go find Jenny."

Sadie Sue didn't move. He patted her head. *"Goot hund."*

Bethany arched one eyebrow. "I see your plan. Jenny stays hidden and you get some work done?"

"It was the dog's idea." He put his tools down. "What are you baking that smells so good?"

"It's a turkey-and-rice casserole for supper. Is your compliment a sly way of asking if you can join us for supper?"

"You read me like a book."

She tipped her head to study him. "I wish that was true."

He looked away first. He would be in deep trouble if she actually could read his mind. At the moment he was wondering what it would be like to kiss her.

"You are always welcome to eat with us, Michael. You never need an invitation." She paused, looking as if she wanted to say something else.

Her indecision vanished. She smiled softly. "If you'll excuse me, I have to go find Jenny."

She clapped her hands together. "Come on, Sadie. Let's leave Michael to finish his work." Sadie rose and followed Bethany out of the room.

Michael picked up his screwdriver but working had lost its appeal. He laid his equipment aside and went out to the kitchen.

Bethany was diligently checking hiding places for her sister. He was the one who happened to notice that the door to the cellar was open a crack.

He clicked his fingers and Sadie trotted to him. He whispered in her ear and then gave her a small push toward the door. She trotted right past her quarry without seeing her. Jenny would've been safe if she hadn't giggled. Sadie spun around and pushed her nose in behind the door.

"Aw, you found me." Jenny patted the dog's head and looked to Michael. "Keep her here while I go hide again."

"Wait a minute." He turned to the refrigerator and opened it. There were several links of cooked sausage left over from breakfast. He picked up the plate and looked at Bethany. "Is it okay if I give this to the dog?"

"Feed *goot* food to a dog? Are you serious?"

"Please?" he cajoled. He used the same tone on Bethany that Jenny had used on him. To his surprise, it worked.

"Very well, but I don't see why the dog needs sausages. She's filled out fine on dog chow."

He motioned to Jenny. "Come here. We are going to teach Sadie Sue to find you so you two can play hide-and-seek and leave me alone."

Bethany's eyes brightened. "That might work. Good thinking. Where did you learn how to train dogs?"

"I've never owned a dog before. This will be trial and error." He crumbled the links into pieces and gave them to Jenny. "Put these in your pocket. When I say 'find Jenny,' I want you to hold out a piece in your hand. Got it?"

"Sure."

"Sadie, find Jenny." Sadie cocked her head to the side as she stared at him.

Jenny fished a piece of sausage out of her pocket and held it out to the dog. "Here, girl."

Sadie never needed a second invitation where food was concerned. She ambled over to Jenny and gently took the piece of meat from her hand.

"That was fine," Michael said. "Now I will take her a little farther away. This time, Jenny, don't say anything. Just hold out your hand."

He took Sadie by the collar and led her to the other side of the room but her eyes were still on the little girl. He turned the dog so she was facing the other way. "Sadie, find Jenny."

Sadie spun around and made a beeline for Jenny, gulped down the piece of meat and barked.

Jenny laughed. "I think that means she wants some more."

"She will have to earn another piece." He took the dog by the collar and led her to the other side of the room.

Bethany regarded him with an amused expression. "You have taught a dog to eat sausage. Everyone will be amazed."

"Don't be a doubting Thomas." This time he took Sadie out into the workroom. "Sadie, find Jenny." The dog galloped from the room straight to Jenny and claimed her tidbit.

He was pleased with his experiment so far. "Now comes the real test. Jenny, I want you to go into the other room where Sadie can't see you. I want you to be quiet. Don't call her. Let's see if she will go look for you."

Jenny hurried out of the room. Bethany smothered a giggle. "I think the command should be 'go find sausage.' If I ever lose my breakfast meat I'll know who to call on. Michael and his amazing Sadie Sue."

"Scoff all you want. This is going to work." He looked down at the dog. "Sadie, find Jenny."

Sadie remained at his side watching him intently with her whole back end wagging. Bethany started laughing. She swung her arm out, pointed toward the doorway and yelled, "Find sausage!" Sadie started barking at her.

As much as he enjoyed the sound of Bethany's laughter, he didn't appreciate her lack of confidence. "She is going to get this. Jenny, come back here."

Jenny walked in the room looking confused. "Did I do it wrong?"

He shook his head. "You did fine. It is Sadie who needs a little more work. Why don't you go put on your coat and boots and we will take this outside, where there aren't so many confusing smells for Sadie and fewer people who want to make fun of her."

Jenny put her arms around Sadie's neck. "You'll get it. I know you will. You're the smartest dog in the whole wide world." Sadie licked her face, making her giggle. Jenny headed for the coatrack. Sadie Sue followed with her nose pressed to Jenny's pocket.

Michael met Bethany's gaze and saw her affection for him in the depths of her eyes. His heart tripped over itself. She cared for him. He knew it as surely as if she spoke the words out loud.

He was falling for this amazing, beautiful, caring woman and he had no idea how to change course.

He had little to offer. He was a broken man. Nothing more than a jumble of pieces like some of the watches that came to him. Sometimes a boxful of gears and a dial couldn't be assembled to work properly no matter how much the owner wanted it repaired.

Bethany tipped her head slightly. "What?"

He shook his head and looked away. "Nothing. I was thinking about a broken watch I received the other day."

"Why does that make you sad?"

"Who said I was sad?"

She leaned closer. "I read you like a book, re-member?"

Then she should be able to see how much he had grown to care for her. "It's sad because the watch can't be fixed."

"Why not?"

He turned away, afraid she could see what he was thinking. "An important part is broken. It can't be mended." He was the broken timepiece and could never forget it.

"Do you think another watch repair business might have the part you need?"

"It's not likely."

"If you really want to restore it, you should ask if someone else can help you. What about asking Mr. Meyers for help?"

Michael heard something in her voice he didn't understand. He looked at her sharply. "What do you know about George Meyers?"

She rubbed her hands together. "He supplied my grandfather with the majority of his work. He also suggested my grandfather write to you and offer you a job here."

Michael tensed. "I told you that."

"I was going through some of Grandfather's things last night and I found the letter George Meyers sent to Grandpa."

Michael swallowed hard. What else was in the letter? "Was it informative?"

"He said you were injured during a robbery at the store."

He shouldn't be surprised. It was newsworthy. "What else did the letter say?"

"That three of his employees were killed by the robbers," she said gently.

He closed his eyes. "That's true."

"I'm so sorry. It must have been terrible for you."

He couldn't speak. Did she pity him now? He couldn't look at her. "What else did George tell your grandfather?"

"Mr. Meyers wanted you to have a chance to start over. I'm glad he asked Grandfather to contact you."

Michael glanced up at her. She meant it. If George had mentioned that Michael was off in the head, Bethany didn't share it. Michael relaxed. George Meyers had given him more than a chance to continue his work. He'd given him a chance at a new life. It had been nearly two weeks since his last PTSD episode. Perhaps he truly was getting better here.

Was his new life one that could include Bethany and the children?

The thought was almost unimaginable. His skin grew clammy. The idea that Bethany might one day love him was terrifyingly wonderful. Was it possible? Did he deserve such a gift? If only he could be sure he would get well.

"I'm ready," Jenny called from the front hall.

"I'll meet you on the back lawn." He was glad of the distraction. He needed to forget about a relationship with Bethany that was anything other than professional. He went out to the workroom, grabbed his coat, pulled on his overshoes and went out the side door with Sadie at his heels. He didn't want Bethany drawn into the darkness that hid inside him, waiting to spring out.

Jenny, dressed in her dark blue coat and bright red mittens, was waiting for him on the snow-covered lawn. She had a red-and-blue knit cap pulled over her white prayer *kapp*. Scooping up some snow, she formed a snowball and tossed it from hand to hand.

"Fetch it, Sadie." Jenny threw the ball, and the dog made a dive for it into a drift, leaving only her back legs and tail visible. She pulled out of the snowbank and shook vigorously, pelting Jenny with clumps of snow. Jenny stumbled and fell. Sadie started licking her face, making Jenny giggle as she tried to fend off the determined pooch. "Stop it, Sadie, stop it."

"She must think you're a sausage," Bethany called from the doorway. She had her arms crossed over her chest and her shoulders hunched against the cold.

Michael packed a snowball and threw it. It smacked against the side of the house above Bethany's head, sending a shower of snow her way. She ducked and brushed the crystals from her clothes. "Hey, that's not fair. I'm not dressed for a snowball fight."

"Then go back inside. Sadie needs to concentrate. You're distracting her." In truth, he was the one distracted by her presence.

"Well, don't expect to get any more sausage from me." She was smiling as she shut the door. A few seconds later he saw her draw the shade aside at the window so she could watch them.

For the next hour he and Jenny worked at teaching Sadie to find the girl. By the time they were both too cold to continue, Sadie was getting it right about half the time. She was still more interested in hunting among the trees than she was in finding Jenny even for a piece of sausage.

"I say we call it quits," Michael said as he sat

down on the back porch steps and rubbed his aching thigh.

"She's almost got it." Jenny sat beside him.

"If we work with her a few more days I think she will find you most times, as long as a rabbit doesn't run in front of her."

Jenny tipped her head to smile at him. "Maybe if I had a rabbit in my pocket instead of sausage she would do better."

"You may be onto something. Where can we get a bunch of pocket-size rabbits?"

"You're funny, Michael."

"You are, too, Jenny."

"Are you going to stay with us a long time?"

He shrugged. "That's a hard question to answer."

"Don't you like it here?"

"Truthfully, I don't like the cold."

"Wait till summer. Then you'll really love it here."

He brushed snow from the top of her hat. "I will be here that long, anyway."

"Why don't you have a wife?"

He leaned back to stare at her. "That's kind of a personal question."

"Well? Why don't you?"

"I guess because I've never met someone that I wanted to marry."

"Gemma says my sister needs to be married

so Ivan can stay here and not have to go live with our *onkel* Harvey."

"I know your sister loves Ivan just like she loves you. But when people get married it has to be because they love each other and not for any other reason."

"You don't have a wife. You could marry Bethany and you'd sort of be my *daed*."

"It's not that simple.

"All the kids in my class have *daeds*. Sometimes they feel sorry for me. There is going to be a father-daughter program in the spring. It would be nice if you could come as my *daed*."

"Jenny, Bethany and I are not going to get married, but I will take you to the father-daughter program anyway. How's that?"

She smiled brightly. "You will?"

"I promise."

"That makes me happy. Can we go in now? My toes are cold."

"Excellent idea. My everything is cold."

She got up and took hold of his hand to pull him to his feet. To his surprise, she hung on to his hand as they walked into the house.

Bethany was sitting beside the window, mending one of Ivan's shirts, when Jenny and Michael came in. "How goes the training?"

"We've decided that to be one hundred percent

effective Jenny must have a rabbit in her pocket when she gets lost. Sadie Sue likes hunting rabbits a little bit more than she likes tracking down Jenny even for a bite of sausage."

The dog, who had been sitting quietly beside Michael, suddenly took off toward the front door. She barked several times when someone knocked.

Bethany got up and went to answer the door. Her *Englisch* neighbor, Greg Janson, tipped his hat. "Good evening, Ms. Martin. I would like a few minutes of your time to discuss something that happened on my farm last night."

A sense of foreboding filled Bethany. "Does this have anything to do with Ivan?"

"In fact it does. I've come to you first. But I'm not opposed to going to the sheriff."

Bethany invited him in. Michael stood in the hallway. Bethany indicated him with one hand. "Michael, this is Greg Janson. He has the farm south of here. Mr. Janson, this is Michael Shetler. He is a business partner."

Mr. Janson nodded. Bethany led the way into the kitchen. "Would you like some coffee, Mr. Janson?"

"No, thank you, ma'am. I'll get right to the point. Last night someone broke into my henhouse and stole three laying hens. The commotion woke my son. He looked out and saw Ivan running down the road with a gunnysack slung over his back."

"If it was nighttime, how was your son able to recognize Ivan?" Michael asked.

"My boy is in the same class as Ivan. He knows him pretty well. They've even been in a scuffle or two together. Plus, the boy was dressed Amish with those flattop black hats you folks prefer."

"I appreciate you coming to me first," Bethany said quietly.

"We have heard a lot of good things about having the Amish for neighbors and for the most part you folks have lived up to your reputation. I don't want to bring the sheriff into this if I don't have to. Things like this can get blown out of proportion. Anybody who has a pig or goat come up missing, they can point a finger at the Amish without any proof. You folks just accept that and forgive the accusers. Nothing gets solved and folks keep on thinking you're guilty. I don't want to see that get started here."

"We appreciate your attitude, Mr. Janson. Would you like to speak to Ivan?" Michael asked.

"I'll leave that up to you."

"I will pay you what the hens are worth." Bethany got up to find her checkbook.

Michael stalled her with a hand to her shoulder. "I'm responsible for Ivan now. I will take care of this."

Mr. Janson held up one hand and shook his head. "I could just as easily have lost them to a lynx or coyote. I don't want to be paid for them. I came here because I want your boy to know that he was seen and that next time he comes on the place I will call the sheriff."

The outside door opened and Ivan came in. He stopped and his eyes grew wide when he saw Mr. Janson. Bethany beckoned to him. "We were just talking about you."

"About me? Why?"

"Because my boy Max saw you stealing our chickens last night," Janson said.

Ivan shook his head. "It wasn't me."

"Max knows you. He was certain."

Ivan looked at Michael. "Honest, I didn't go out last night. Why would I take chickens?"

Michael laid a hand on Ivan's shoulder. "Do you know who might have done it?"

Ivan stared down at his feet. "I only know it wasn't me."

Bethany turned to Mr. Janson. "Thank you for bringing this to our attention."

"Like I said, I don't want it to get out of hand." He tipped his hat to her and left.

Bethany waited until the door closed and then she turned to Ivan. "How could you do something so foolish?"

"I knew you wouldn't believe me."

Michael kept his hand on Ivan's shoulder. "I believe you. Why would someone want to make it look like you are the one who took them?"

"I don't know."

"But you do have an idea who it was, don't you?"

Ivan turned his pleading eyes to Michael. "I can't tell. I promised I wouldn't tell."

Chapter Ten

Bethany was shocked that Michael believed Ivan. Even she doubted her brother's innocence. Yet the crime didn't make any sense. Why would Ivan steal three chickens?

Why would anyone? The vast majority of farms in the area had their own chickens as she did.

"Go on and get ready for supper, Ivan." When her brother left the room, Bethany looked at Michael. "What are we going to do with him?"

"The next time there is a report about something Ivan is suspected of doing, I think it would be best to involve the police."

"The bishop would not agree to that. Our community has taken great pains to avoid any involvement by the *Englisch* law."

"The police can easily rule out Ivan as a suspect by fingerprints or by DNA. Their findings will carry weight with the *Englisch* community."

"You really think someone is deliberately blaming Ivan?"

"I do."

She wished she could be so positive. This setback was crushing. "I'm not sure I can simply wait for another incident to occur."

"It's the only choice we have unless Ivan can be convinced to break his promise and tells us what he knows."

"Do you know who he's protecting?"

"I think I do but I have no proof. I think you know, too."

"Jeffrey?"

He nodded. She shook her head in bewilderment. "But why? Do you think we should tell the bishop about this?"

Michael took his time answering her. "I'd rather not, but if you feel you should, then I'm okay with it."

"What do we do?"

"We keep to a normal pattern of activity. And we keep a good eye on Ivan. What are your plans for this week?"

"I have a lot of things that need to be done. Christmas is getting closer by the minute. I have a ton of baking to get finished. On Saturday I plan to send the children out to collect fir branches and winterberries for the house and for wreaths. I was hoping that you would go with them."

"I can."

"On Sunday Pastor Frank is coming to supper."

"Why?" He looked at her suspiciously.

"Because he's a friend. We enjoyed his company. He frequently drives us and other Amish people in his van at no charge."

"I see."

She walked to the window and stared out at the low gray clouds scuttling across the sky. A few snowflakes floated down from them. She wound the ribbon of her *kapp* around one finger. "I had asked Frank to speak with Ivan about his behavior but I never took Ivan to see him. He's been doing so much better lately. You have been a good influence on him. But now this."

Michael walked up to stand behind her. She could see their reflection together in the window. She was becoming dependent on him for advice and for comfort. She longed to rest her head against his shoulder and feel she wasn't facing this problem alone.

"I know you're worried," he said quietly.

If she leaned back, would he take her in his arms? It was a foolish thought. "To worry is to doubt God's mercy. I try not to, but it seems to be my best talent."

He chuckled. "I thought speaking Cow was your best talent."

She smiled. "Don't tell Frank I get my advice

from Clarabelle. He went to many years of school to become a psychologist and counselor so he could advise folks."

"Jenny thinks you should marry. That way Ivan won't be sent away."

Bethany looked down as her face grew hot. "She's been listening to Gemma. Husbands don't exactly grow on trees in New Covenant."

"Anyone you chose would be getting a fine wife."

She looked up to study his reflection in the glass but it wasn't clear enough to let her see what he was thinking. "Are you making me an offer?"

"You would be getting a very poor bargain if I was."

She turned around so she could look into his eyes. "Why do you say that?"

"Because it's the truth."

There was so much pain in his voice and deep in his eyes that she wanted to hold him and promise to make everything better. She couldn't. She knew that, but it didn't lessen her desire to help him.

The letter from Mr. Meyers hadn't told her why Michael didn't return to work in his store or why he left his family in Ohio to come to Maine. He could have easily fixed watches for Mr. Meyers there the same way he was doing here. "What's wrong, Michael?"

He laid a hand against her cheek. "Nothing that you can fix."

"How do I know that if you can't tell me what troubles you?"

"Trust me. You don't want to know." He turned and walked down the hall and out the back door.

He was so wrong. She wanted to know everything about Michael Shetler. Her mother's voice echoed from the past. *If you don't know a man inside and out, don't marry him. He'll bring you nothing but pain.*

Michael was up early on Saturday because he knew Ivan and Jenny would be over as soon as they could. He hoped that Bethany would accompany them on their trek into the woods to gather winterberries and fir boughs for wreath making but he wasn't sure that she would. It was hard for him to believe that he had only been in New Covenant a little over two weeks. So much had happened. So much had changed. He hadn't had a flashback for thirteen days and not a single panic attack. Maybe his PTSD episodes were behind him for good. He prayed it was true.

Sadie alerted him that the children had arrived by scratching at the door and woofing softly. He opened the door and she shot outside, barking and bounding around Jenny. The girl was pulling a red toboggan. She dropped to her knees and threw her arms around Sadie's neck. The dog responded by licking her face. Jenny's giggle was so much like Bethany's that anyone could tell they were related. Ivan stopped to pet the dog, too.

Bethany came up the hill behind the children. Her bright welcoming smile was like the sun breaking through on a dreary day. He was happy to see her smiling again after the depressing visit with Mr. Janson.

Michael's refusal to talk about his past troubled her, too. He knew that, but his decision would never change.

Bethany pulled a blue toboggan with a bushel basket on it. Like the children, she was bundled for the outdoors with a heavy coat, mittens and snow boots. The red-and-white-striped knit scarf around her neck was identical to the one Jenny was wearing.

Ivan patted Sadie and then hurried to Michael's door. He was pulling a yellow disk sled. "*Guder mariye*, Michael."

"Morning, Ivan. So where are we going?"

The boy pointed up the ridge. "I know the perfect place to get pine boughs. It isn't far."

Michael looked at the pine-covered forest stretching up into the mountains. "I hope that's true. I'm not sure my leg will hold up in all this snow. Besides, don't we have about a million trees to choose from close to home?"

"It has to be balsam fir and we will pull you on the sled if you get tired." Bethany stopped beside Ivan.

"I give up. Why balsam?" Michael returned her smile. The darkness of his past was etched deep in his soul, but just being with her gave him hope that he could be healed. He prayed that God would show him mercy.

Michael couldn't plan any kind of family life until he was sure, but he could dream of the day when he had the right to tell Bethany how he felt about her.

"I want balsam fir because of its wonderful, spicy scent, its lovely color and its short dense needles."

Michael looked at both of their sleds. "Are we planning to bring back a lot of branches? I was thinking we'd have an armful or two."

Bethany began counting on her fingers. "Gemma and her mother want some. We need enough for our house and for your cabin. Plus, I will make some for friends and I also plan to sell a few at the grocer's. Mr. Meriwether lets us set up a display in front of his store. Last year I sold thirty-eight of them and made almost a thousand dollars."

"I didn't know you operated a seasonal business."

"We have to make ends meet any way we can. Are you ready?"

He nodded even though he wasn't looking forward to the hike. Sadie Sue took off after a rabbit.

Ivan put Jenny on her sled and pulled her along as he walked beside Michael. Ivan met Michael's gaze. "The snow might get too deep for her. A man takes care of his family, right?"

Michael smiled. "Right."

When Sadie Sue returned without a bunny, Jenny coaxed her to sit on the sled with her. She and Ivan took turns pulling the dog along. Sadie wasn't sure she liked the ride and kept jumping off and then back on. Their antics had Michael and Bethany laughing as they made their way up into the forest.

Ivan was true to his word. He led them to a small grove of the fir trees less than three hundred yards beyond Michael's cabin. The trees were almost all the same size at about eight feet tall and evenly spaced.

Michael glanced at Bethany. "Someone planted this grove. Do we have permission to harvest these?"

She gave him a reassuring grin. "We do. This land belongs to Pastor Frank. We are free to use what we like. If we take a whole tree, he asks that we replant one to replace it."

"He's a generous man." Michael hadn't seen him since the night of his flashback. Although he had been tempted to attend the survivors' group meeting, he wasn't ready to have others know about his problem.

Bethany distributed clippers to everyone and they set about filling the sleds with piles of the wonderfully pungent branches. When the children had finished cutting, they went exploring while the adults cinched down the loads with lengths of rope.

Michael tied off the last knot, dusted the snow from a nearby fallen log and sat down to rest. Bethany came over to join him. The view spread out before them was breathtaking. They could see the winding course of the river down below, the silver ribbon of highway that paralleled the river's course and the houses of Fort Craig. In the distance the Appalachian mountain range provided a beautiful backdrop. It was a lovely spot and he had a beautiful woman beside him.

She rubbed her hands up and down on her arms. "It's getting colder."

He slipped his arm around her and she moved closer, making his heart beat faster. Not with fear but with joy.

"How long have you been taking care of your brother and sister?" Michael asked gently. He leaned forward to see her face.

Bethany smiled. "A long time."

"What happened to your parents? Does it bother you to talk about it?"

She shook her head. "My mother passed away shortly after Jenny was born. The doctor had a medical reason but I think she died of a broken heart. My father had left us about a month before that."

"I don't understand."

"Neither did I. If you are thinking that my father died, you are mistaken. My father packed up and moved away. He didn't want to be Amish anymore. It was the third time he had come back into our lives, begged for forgiveness, and was welcomed by our Amish community. I would like to give him credit for trying to shoulder his responsibilities, but I'm not sure he tried very hard."

"He left your mother twice before that? Left her and his children?" Michael could barely believe what he was hearing.

"The first time he went away I was six. I woke up on my sixth birthday to find my mother crying and my father gone. Just gone. He didn't bother to tell me goodbye."

"I'm sorry. That was cruel."

"He came back two years later, said he was sorry and begged Mother to give him another chance. She did. I was overjoyed. Mother was, too, but only for a while. He stayed for three years but even as a child I could see they weren't happy together. He left again. The next time he came back he only stayed a year."

"Did he ever tell you why he couldn't stay or what he did when he was away?"

"Not to me. He refused to talk about his other life. He did come to Mother's funeral. I thought he would take care of us but he said he couldn't. I was sixteen. He left me with a brokenhearted little boy and a newborn babe. We haven't seen or heard from him since."

"It's hard to believe a man could cast aside his responsibilities that way." No wonder she was so committed to keeping the children with her.

"Fortunately, our mother's father, Elijah, stepped up to take us in. My father's brother, Onkel Harvey, was willing to accept us but I wanted to stay with Grandpa. That's how I ended up helping Elijah look for a place to start his new Amish community. Each fall after the farm work was done, we would travel to different locations, looking for a place to settle. When we received a letter from Pastor Frank telling us about New Covenant, we decided to visit during the winter to see just how bad it was going to be. The road leading to our farm was merely a tunnel plowed through four feet of snow."

"I'm sorry about your father."

"Our faith requires a strength of character that he didn't possess. My mother could have gone with him, but she refused to abandon her faith and break her vows to God."

"She must've been a strong woman."

"She was, but each time my father came back and then left again, it was like he took pieces of her strength with him until there was nothing left."

"You have inherited your strength from her."

"I hope so. She wanted Father to come back so badly. She prayed for it. When she knew she was dying, she made me promise I would keep the family together. She didn't say she wanted it for him in case he came back, but I think that's exactly what she hoped for."

"It was a big burden to place on a young girl." He bent and kissed her lips gently.

He felt her sharp intake of breath and he drew back. "Maybe I shouldn't have done that."

"I didn't mind."

He looked away from the comfort she offered. "Did you ever consider leaving the Amish?"

"I think we all question at one time or another if this path to God is the right one for us. I never seriously considered leaving. What about you?"

"I did more than question. I left the Amish life behind and lived in the outside world for five years."

She gave him a funny look. "You did? What made you come back?"

"That is not something I care to talk about." His answer seemed to take her by surprise.

"I'm sorry. I'm just trying to understand. You say you want to live alone but you spend almost as much time with my family as I do."

"Ivan and Jenny can be hard to resist." As was their big sister. He rose to his feet and held out his hand to her. "We should head back."

"Will you remain Amish?"

He could tell it was important to her to know the answer. "I will."

Bethany allowed him to help her up but she pulled her hand away from his quickly. She had shared the most painful part of her life but he was unwilling to speak of his past. Until this moment she considered him someone she could count on. Someone dependable, but was he? He'd left the Amish once. What if he decided to leave again? A seed of doubt had been sown in her mind.

She shouldn't have let him kiss her. There was no promise between them. No plan for the future. That knowledge alone should help keep her emotions from carrying her away where he was concerned.

Ivan came through the trees with a big bundle of winterberry branches in his arms, leaving a thin trail of red berries on the snow behind him. Sadie Sue walked beside him. He laid the branches on top of the blue sled. Bethany looked around. "Where is Jenny?"

"She said she wanted to play hide-and-seek with Sadie Sue. She's gone to hide."

Michael patted the dog's head. "Let's hope she has a bunny in her pocket."

Bethany didn't look amused. "Let's pray we can find her if the dog can't."

"That will be easy. We'll just follow her footsteps in the snow," Ivan said.

Michael took Sadie Sue's head between his hands. "Find Jenny."

Sadie took off into the trees. He looked at Bethany. "Do we follow the dog or just hope she finds Jenny before it gets dark?"

"I'm going to follow the dog." She pointed to the log they had been sitting on. "You don't need to do more hiking than you have already. Rest."

Ivan sat on the log. "I'm going to wait here."

They heard Sadie barking in the distance. Bethany started toward the sound. She hadn't gone far when she saw Jenny and the dog coming toward her. Jenny was covered with snow but she was smiling from ear to ear. "She found me. I buried myself under the snow and she found me. She's the smartest dog in the whole wide world."

Bethany smiled at her sister. "Well, for that she deserves a whole sausage. Are you ready to go home?"

Jenny nodded and they began to walk side by side. She glanced up at Bethany. "Can I ask you something?"

"Sure."

"I've been thinking that you should marry Michael."

Bethany arched one eyebrow. "You've been thinking that, have you?"

Jenny cocked her head to the side as a serious expression settled over her face. "I like him. Ivan wouldn't have to go away and you could have babies."

"I see you have this all figured out. How many babies do you think I should have?"

"Three or four. Mostly girls but you could have one boy if you wanted to."

It hurt Bethany's heart to know her little sister was worrying about Ivan, too. She managed a reassuring smile. "I don't believe the bishop is going to send Ivan away, so I'm not going to marry Michael or anyone else until you and Ivan are grown up. You are my family. I don't need anyone else."

Jenny kicked at the snow. "Ivan said you would say that."

Bethany patted her sister on the head. "Then Ivan is smarter than I gave him credit for."

On Sunday evening Michael was reading Elijah's book on the history of clocks when Sadie perked up and thumped her tail on the floor. She kept her eyes on the front door. A knock followed. Michael knew who was there before he opened the door.

"Good evening, Frank."

"Evening, Michael. I thought I would stop by and see if I could interest you in a game of chess." He had a case under his arm.

"I have a strong suspicion that I'll be outclassed, but sure, come in."

Frank looked at Sadie. "Is this the same dog you had before?"

"It is."

He bent to pat her head. "Living with you certainly agrees with her. I don't see a single rib sticking out anymore. Her coat is gorgeous. Such a pretty golden color." He glanced at Michael. "How have you been?"

Michael led the way to a small table and two chairs set in the corner. He clicked on the floor lamp and took a seat. "Sadie is not the only one improving. I've come a long way."

"Really?" Frank opened his case and lifted out a chessboard and pieces. "Tell me about it."

"I haven't had a flashback or a panic attack since the last time we spoke. I've never gone so long without an episode."

Frank glanced at Michael. "I'm glad to hear it.

I've been expecting you to show up at one of my support groups but you keep disappointing me."

"I don't see the need for therapy if I'm getting better on my own. You said some people get over it by themselves."

"I did say that. What do you think has made the difference?"

"Sadie Sue, for one thing. She always alerts me if someone is near. I depend on her sharp nose and ears. If I start getting edgy, she will come over and distract me. She's amazing."

"So instead of being hypervigilant, you rely on the dog to do that for you. I don't want to belittle your progress, but isn't that substituting one kind of crutch for another?"

"Maybe it is but it makes life bearable."

"Bethany tells me Ivan has been in trouble again but that you are sticking up for the boy." Frank began to place the chess pieces on the board.

"I think the saying is 'innocent until proven guilty.'"

"Sadly that is sometimes forgotten in today's society. Have you thought more about your flashback triggers?"

Michael shifted uncomfortably in his chair. "Like I told you, I haven't had one since the night we met."

"I'm glad to see you are improving but I hope

you understand that recovery is a slow process. There will be setbacks. They may not be as severe as what you've had in the past but you should be prepared for them. Being prepared ahead of time makes it easier for you and for anyone with you to get through an episode. Black or white?" He held out two chess pieces.

"White. How can I be prepared for one if I never know when they will occur?" Michael positioned his men on the board.

"That's a good question. Since you are working and living close to Bethany, she might benefit from learning about this, too."

Michael glanced up sharply. "I don't want her involved."

"Is that wise? She has a good head on her shoulders. She won't panic."

"No!"

"Okay, but I think you're making a mistake."

"It's mine to make." He was aware of Bethany's withdrawal at the pine branch gathering. Was it because of his kiss or something else? It had been hard for her to relate the story of how her father bounced in and out of her life and then abandoned them. When Michael admitted that he had left the Amish once before, it touched a nerve for her.

Maybe her coolness was for the best. He was

better. He knew he was better, but he wasn't sure if it would last.

After beginning the game in silence and playing for a while, Michael realized he wasn't outclassed by Pastor Frank. They were evenly matched and he began to enjoy the game.

"Do you have plans for next Saturday evening?" Frank asked.

"Nope. Why?"

"The city of Presque Isle puts on a holiday parade every year that's worth going to see. I'm getting together a vanload of Amish folks and driving them up to enjoy it. Would you like to join us?"

A big outing, crowds—he wasn't sure he was up to it. "Is it something Ivan and Jenny would enjoy?"

"Absolutely. It's fun for all ages and it's free. I've already asked Bethany and she said she would come."

"I'll consider it. I believe this is checkmate." Michael moved his queen to trap Frank's king.

Frank studied the board and sighed heavily. "I concede. Nice game."

"Another?" Michael asked.

Frank shook his head. "I should get going. I'll save you a seat in the van if you decide to go with us. Think about what I've said. Being prepared to endure a flashback or panic attack can make it easier on everyone involved."

"I'll keep it in mind."

But he wouldn't involve Bethany. Not ever.

Chapter Eleven

Bethany lifted Jenny to stand on a chair. The girl was wearing her Christmas costume and Bethany wanted to make sure the hem was straight. "Hold your arms out," she mumbled around the three straight pins she held between her lips. Two dozen more were stuck into the pincushion shaped like a tomato that she wore on her wrist.

The house smelled of pine and cinnamon. Green boughs graced the window ledges and the fireplace mantel. Christmas cards from faraway friends had started arriving. They were displayed nestled in the pine branches or hung from red yarn stretched across the windows. Christmas was fast approaching, and in spite of her assurance to Jenny, Bethany's last hope of keeping Ivan had crumbled. Her uncle had included a letter in his Christmas card. He strongly believed the bishop was right and Ivan should return with him. It was a bitter blow. It seemed to be God's will to separate her family.

She folded the material of the white gown under and pinned it across the top of Jenny's feet. "Is this how long you want it?"

"I don't know," Jenny said quietly.

"Did the play director tell you if you had to have wings?"

"I can't be an angel without wings."

"But you are the narrator. Should your costume be different than the other angels or the same?"

Jenny put her arms down. "I don't know." Her lower lip trembled.

Bethany took a hold of her sister's hand. "Don't cry. This is for your Christmas pageant. This should be fun. I'll make it long enough to touch the floor and if the director says it should be shorter then I will shorten it. You don't have dress rehearsal for a few days, so I have plenty of time to change it."

"Good thinking." Michael stood in the open doorway to his workroom. "If you cut it too short you won't be able to lengthen it."

She rolled her eyes at him. "Have you had a lot of experience as a seamstress?"

Michael had been joining the conversations more often in the past few days. The workroom door hadn't been closed all week. She welcomed his interactions with her family but she couldn't forget the all-too-brief kiss they'd shared. What did it mean? Did it mean anything to him? During his time in the outside world, had he kissed lots of women?

"As a matter of fact, I have had some sewing experience," he declared. "My brother and I made a camel costume for our Christmas pageant when I was in the sixth grade. We were told it was very lifelike."

Bethany looked around for her fabric marker and realized she had left it in the sewing room. "I'll be right back, Jenny."

She left the room, grabbed the marker from the sewing machine and started back into the kitchen. She was in the hall when she heard Michael say, "Of course you can ask me anything, Jenny. What's wrong?"

Bethany waited in the hall to hear what Jenny had to say. Why was her sister confiding in Michael instead of in her?

"I don't want to be the narrator," Jenny said.

"You don't? Why not? I think you will make a fine narrator."

"Mrs. Whipple says my voice is too small. I didn't know I had a small voice. How do I get a bigger one?"

"I don't think there's anything wrong with your voice, Jenny. Who is Mrs. Whipple?"

"She's one of the ladies helping our director,

Miss Carson. I heard her tell Miss Carson that someone else should be the narrator because she couldn't hear me in the back row."

"That made you feel bad, didn't it?"

Bethany didn't hear anything. She assumed Jenny was nodding.

"Jenny, I will be happy to help you make your voice bigger."

"You will?" Jenny sounded thrilled.

"Absolutely. We will practice once your sister is finished with your costume. Just come into the workroom when the two of you are done."

"I'm not supposed to bother you in the workroom."

He chuckled. "That's only when the door is closed. When the door is open you can come in whenever you like."

Bethany walked into the kitchen and saw Jenny had her arms around Michael's neck. He pulled her arms away as a fierce blush stained his cheeks.

"I have to get back to work," he mumbled.

He was so good with children. He should have a dozen of his own.

When she realized where her thoughts were taking her, she pushed them aside. He wasn't the one for her. How could she consider a relationship with someone whose past was so full of secrets, with a man who didn't feel he could confide in her?

* * *

Michael closed the cover of a grandmother clock after setting the time. He waited as it ticked its way to the top of the hour. The chimes rang out in clear pure tones. He wiped his fingerprints from the glass. Tomorrow he would pack it up and mail it back to George Meyers. His former boss had been sending a steady stream of work his way, and Michael was grateful.

Jenny appeared in the doorway. "Can I come in?"

"Sure."

She came in and climbed up on his work stool. She opened the drawer and lifted out one of the tools. "Will one of these tools make my voice bigger?"

He smiled and took the pliers from her. "We will save those as a last resort. You stand on a stage, don't you?"

She nodded. He lifted her onto the workbench. "There are a few things you have to do to get a bigger voice. Right now, I want you to close your eyes. And I want you to whisper your first two lines."

Movement caught his eye and he glanced over to see Bethany watching him. He beckoned her to come in. She did but she stayed by the door.

"How was that?" Jenny asked.

"Fine. I want you to keep your eyes closed and

pretend you need Ivan to come in from the other room. He's pretty far away but you can't yell. Want to try it? Talk loud. Say your lines."

"Ivan, a long time ago, in a land far away, there were shepherds tending their flocks in the hills near the little town of Bethlehem. Can you hear me?"

"That's pretty good. Now I want you to try telling him again but this time he is upstairs."

She shook her head. "I don't think he can hear me upstairs."

"Bethany, will you go to the stairwell and see if you can hear Jenny?"

"Of course." She turned and walked out of the room.

Jenny repeated her lines in a loud voice. A few moments later Bethany returned.

"Well?" Michael looked at Bethany for confirmation.

"I heard her, but just barely."

"Hmm. I wonder what will help. Bethany, do you have any suggestions?"

They conferred and with some practice they were able to get Jenny to be heard by someone standing on the stairwell. Jenny was excited that she wouldn't have to give up being the narrator and promised to speak loud enough to be heard on the roof. As she went to change out of her costume, Bethany stayed in the workroom.

She opened one of the drawers. "I've often wondered what all these things are for."

He sensed that she wanted to talk about something else. He would let her work up her courage. "It looks like a lot of stuff but there are just different sizes of the same items. Gears and pins. Pliers and screwdrivers. Tweezers and little magnets to retrieve dropped pieces of metal."

She picked up his jeweler's loupe. "And this is to let you see things more clearly, isn't it?" She held it to her eye and turned so she was looking at him.

"Is it working?" he asked gently.

"I'm not sure." She pulled it away from her face. "Every time I look I see something different." He knew she was talking about him.

"That is one of the drawbacks of looking too closely."

"I think the problem is I didn't have my subject in focus. What can I do about that?"

"Not much, I'm afraid, if your subject is unwilling to cooperate." He wasn't ready to risk her knowing the whole truth.

"So the loupe is for seeing small pieces in great detail. How do I see the whole picture in greater detail?"

"The trick is to take a step back," he said bluntly. Their relationship had progressed so quickly he wasn't sure of his own feelings or of hers.

She laid the lens down. "I think that's what I need to do."

"I think it would be best if we both did that."

A wry smile curved her lips. "I agree."

She started to walk past him but he caught her arm. "Can we still be friends?"

"I don't see why not," she replied, but he couldn't tell if she meant it.

Bethany expected her next meeting with Michael would be awkward. To prolong the inevitable, she went to visit her friend Gemma after the kids were off to school the following morning.

Gemma welcomed her with a hug and then intense scrutiny. "Okay, out with it. What's troubling you?"

Bethany turned away from her friend's sharp eyes. "The same thing. Ivan." It was true but it wasn't the whole truth.

"I know you are worried about your brother but something else is on your mind or you wouldn't be here."

Bethany began to remove her bonnet and coat. "You make it sound like I never come to see you unless I'm in some kind of crisis."

Gemma poured two cups of coffee and sat down at the table with them. She pushed one across to Bethany when she sat down. "You visit me without a crisis often, but I know you well enough to see you are deeply troubled. What is it? I'm here to help."

Bethany prided herself on being in control. She didn't believe women were weaker than men, but when she looked up and saw the sympathy in Gemma's eyes, Bethany's pride flew out the window. Tears welled up and spilled down her cheeks. "I'm so confused."

"Oh, you poor dear." Gemma was around the table in a moment and gathered Bethany into her arms. "It's okay. Go ahead and cry."

"I can't abide women who act like watering cans." She sniffled and continued to cry.

Gemma patted Bethany's back. "No one could accuse you of being a watering can. You are one of the strongest women I have ever had the privilege to know."

"Then why do I feel like such a fool?" Bethany wailed.

"Because love makes glorious fools of us all."

"I'm not in love. I can't be in love."

"And yet here you are crying on my shoulder because your mystery man has stolen your heart."

Bethany drew back to stare at Gemma in amazement. "How can you know that?"

"Because I have been in love myself."

"You have? With who?"

"A fellow who is denser than a post. But never

mind about me. This is about you. First I have to know how bad it is. Has he kissed you?"

Bethany buried her face in her hands and nodded, unable to speak.

"Did you kiss him back?"

"Maybe just a little," she whispered.

"Do Ivan and Jenny like him?"

"Jenny adores him. Ivan looks up to him and tries to emulate him."

"All right. Has he told you that he loves you?"

"*Nee*, we've not spoken of our feelings."

"So you haven't professed your love. Okay. Things aren't as bad as you are making them out to be."

"How can you say that? I spend my days and nights thinking about him, wondering if he's thinking about me."

"That's normal in any new relationship. I know that you are a wonderful catch for any man. I don't see the problem on this end. Why is he all wrong for you?"

Bethany wiped her face with both hands and drew a ragged breath. "Because I don't know anything about him."

"You know a lot of things about him."

"You don't understand. Something bad happened to him. He has told me in general terms what happened but I know there is something else. Something he won't talk about. He's so secretive. I'm worried that I really may not want to know what he did."

"Bethany, you have to ask yourself what is the one sin that you can't forgive."

She frowned slightly as she looked at Gemma. "There is no sin that cannot be forgiven."

"You believe that with all your heart, don't you?"

"Of course I do. Jesus died on the cross for all men's sins. We are instructed by God to forgive those that have trespassed against us."

"What is the one thing in Michael's past that you could not forgive?"

That made her pause. "I would forgive anything."

"Then why do you have to know what he has done?"

Bethany pulled her coffee mug close and took a sip. It was lukewarm. "It's not that I can't forgive his sins great or small. It's that I believe you can't love someone that you don't trust. How can he love me if he doesn't trust me enough to share his burdens?"

"Has he said that he loves you?"

"*Nee*, he has not."

"But you are in love with him?"

Bethany gave her friend a beseeching glance. "Maybe. I don't know. What would you do in my place?"

"Sell the farm and move to someplace warm."

Bethany managed a half-hearted smile. "You know I'm being serious."

"I do. I trust your judgment, Bethany. Therefore, you should trust your own judgment. You have so many things vying for your attention and that keeps you from thinking straight. You and I both know that you won't marry anyone before Christmas, even if it is the only way to keep Ivan with you. You're much too smart for that. An Amish marriage is forever. Ivan will return to us when he is older. It will be a hard separation, but it won't be forever. If you like Michael Shetler, even if you think you love him, you still need time to get to know one another."

"He asked me if we could be friends."

"Did he mean it?"

Bethany thought back to that moment. "I believe he did."

"That's a good sign. It means he cares about you and he values the relationship the two of you have. What did you say?"

"I said I didn't see why not."

"Well, that should give him some hope. Can you be his friend even if he never confides in you?"

Bethany pondered the question. She liked Michael. More than that, she cared deeply about him. He made her laugh. He understood Ivan better than she ever could. Jenny adored him and looked up to him. Bethany realized her life would be poorer if Michael Shetler wasn't in it. If his friendship was all that she could have, she would gladly hold on to it.

She nodded. "I can be his friend. You, Gemma, are such a wise friend. You give much better advice than Clarabelle."

Gemma looked appalled. "I should hope so. Isn't that your milk cow?"

Bethany chuckled. "Someday I will tell you the story. I will take your advice. I won't rush into anything. I still believe that Ivan is better off with me. I'm not letting him go without a fight."

Gemma took a sip of her coffee and made a bitter face. "That sounds like the Bethany I know and love. How about a fresh cup of hot coffee?"

"And a lemon cookie?"

"Absolutely. They come free with all my advice. How would you like to stay and help me bake cookies for the holidays? I need eight dozen."

"I would be delighted to repay even a small portion of your kindness."

Bethany spent the entire day with Gemma, enjoying her friendship, sampling new cookie recipes and making several dozen of each type to take home. Chocolate chip cookies, oatmeal cookies, gingerbread men, moose munch, sugar cookies and lemon crisps because she knew Michael would enjoy them. With several large plastic containers in her arms, she paused outside Gemma's front door.

"Thank you again."

Gemma waved aside Bethany's gratitude. "Someday I will need your shoulder to cry on."

"It will be available day or night. Are you going with Pastor Frank to see the Christmas parade in town?"

"I am. So are my folks. What about you?"

"The children and I are going for sure. I don't know about Michael."

"We will enjoy it with him or without him, right?"

"Right."

Bethany waved goodbye and headed home. As she approached her lane, she saw the school bus pull away. Four of the local schoolchildren went swarming up the mounds of snow left by the snowplows on her side of the road. She noticed Jeffrey was one of them but she didn't see Ivan.

She stopped to watch them playing king of the mountain. The one who obtained the summit then had to keep others from claiming his throne. There was more pushing and shoving than she liked to see, but all she did was caution them.

"Make sure you don't push anyone toward the road. Stay on the outside of those piles."

"We know, Ms. Martin," one of the younger boys replied.

She left them to their fun and walked up her drive. Pastor Frank's van sat parked in front of the house. The sound of laughter and the smell of pizza greeted her as she entered. She stepped into the kitchen to see Pastor Frank, Michael, Ivan and Jenny seated around the table, making Christmas wreaths. All of them wore pine branch crowns around their heads. Michael's held two long branches upright like antlers. Jenny had two small upright branches near the front of her head. Ivan had two bushy branches hanging down. The pastor had red winterberries woven into his.

Bethany shook her head. "What is going on in here?"

"We're making Christmas wreaths to sell at the market," Jenny said.

Bethany set down her containers of cookies. "I see. Who are you supposed to be?" she asked, looking askew at all of them.

"I'm a bunny," Jenny said with a giggle. She got down from the table and hopped around the room.

Ivan slid off his chair. "I'm a hound dog." He started barking and chasing Jenny. Sadie Sue immediately got up from her place under the table and started barking at them as they ran up the stairs with her close on their heels.

Bethany looked at Michael and tried not to laugh. "I assume you are a Christmas reindeer?"

He shook his head, making one of his antlers fall off. He picked it up and tucked it in again. "I am a Maine moose."

"Of course you are. Pastor Frank?"

"I'm a pastor with a limited imagination wearing a pine branch wreath on my head decorated by Jenny." He gave her a big smile.

She looked at the number of wreaths stacked against the wall. "You have been busy. I know the children just got home a little while ago, so, Michael, did you make these by yourself or did Frank help you?"

"Those were all done by Michael," the pastor said. "I just brought the pizza. It's baking now. You are always feeding me. I thought I'd return the favor."

Michael stretched his neck one way and then the other. "I was tired of fixing clocks and decided to try my hand at wreath making. What do you think?"

She picked up several and checked the construction. "Not bad at all. I'm sure these will sell well with a little more decoration added."

"Did you have a good day?" he asked with a shade of uncertainty in his eyes.

She smiled. "I did. I went to visit Gemma and we baked cookies all day."

"Are there samples?" Pastor Frank's gaze slid to the counter and her plastic containers.

"There are. Pastor Frank, I know you enjoy oatmeal cookies. I have two dozen set aside just for you." She handed him a full plastic baggie.

"These are going straight out to my van so I don't forget them later." He removed his crown before heading out the door.

Bethany held out a container. "I actually made some moose munch if you want to try that, Michael the Moose."

He got up from his chair. "You don't have to ask me twice."

Opening one of the containers, he took a handful of the mix and turned to face her with his hip leaning against the counter. "How are you today?" he asked.

She cocked her head slightly. "I'm better. I had a wonderful time with Gemma and I've come to realize how truly valuable a great friendship can be."

"Present company excluded?" he asked.

"Present company included," she assured him. His smile warmed her all the way through.

Pastor Frank returned a few minutes later. The children thundered down the stairs when he called out that the pizza was ready. Bethany smiled as they crowded around him eagerly. This was the way it had been before her grandfather died. Friends stopping by. Storytelling, good food and good company. It was comforting to know it didn't have to change.

After supper Bethany and Jenny rehearsed her lines as the men decided to teach Ivan the game of chess. The boy had an aptitude for it and was soon intent on learning more moves. It was almost ten thirty when Bethany called a stop to the game.

"It's a school night and it is way past Ivan's bedtime." She had tucked Jenny in hours ago.

Pastor Frank pulled on his coat. "I apologize for keeping you all up so late. It was like old times and I guess I got carried away. Good night, all."

Bethany and Michael watched him leave from the doorway. When he drove out of sight, she closed the door.

"I'd better leave, too," Michael said. "I had a fine time tonight, Bethany. I've forgotten how satisfying an ordinary night with friends can be."

"I'm glad you enjoyed yourself. We'll do it again soon."

He put on his hat and coat, but instead of leaving he seemed to come to some decision. "The weather isn't bad and I've been sitting too long. Would you care to take a walk with me?"

"That would be nice." She put on her coat and

gloves and walked out the door to stand beside him. "Which way?"

"You have lived here longer than I have. You choose the direction."

"There is a path that leads to an overlook. It's not too steep."

"I'll keep up. Don't worry about me."

She took him at his word. They walked in silence for a time with Sadie Sue ambling alongside Michael. The crunch of their boots in the snow was the only sound. It was cold, but Bethany was warmly dressed and exercise kept her from getting chilled. "What do you think of New Covenant?" It was a safe subject and she was interested in his opinion.

"It's a long way from being a self-supportive community."

"What do you think we need here?"

"You don't have a blacksmith or wheelwright."

"We have a blacksmith coming in the spring. A man with three boys."

"You don't have an Amish school."

"Once we reach ten school-age children in the community, the bishop will allow us to hire a teacher and open a school of our own."

"You need a grocer. Mr. Meriwether's prices are too high."

She chuckled. "Tell me something I don't know. I shop there every week."

"And where is the nearest pizza parlor? What is an Amish settlement without a pizza parlor?"

"There is one in Fort Craig. They even deliver."

"I'll have to get their number. What about you, Bethany? What do you want out of New Covenant?"

"I want to see a happy, healthy, thriving community. We are so few and far between right now. I pray the community survives."

"And if that doesn't happen? What if there is a split in the church? It happens all the time. You won't be immune because of your remoteness."

She shrugged. "I guess we'll just have to face that issue when it comes, if it comes. I like to expect the best that life has to offer."

"Isn't it better to expect the worst and then be pleased when it doesn't show up?"

"I reckon you and I simply look at life differently. Here is the overlook I mentioned. I don't see anyone around now, but it's a popular place with young lovers in the spring and summer."

They came out onto a rock ledge that jutted out between two old pine trees. Below was a stunning view of the Aroostook River. It was a silver ribbon winding its way through the countryside illuminated by a full moon just rising. She pointed east. "See where the farmland stops and the forest starts?"

"I do."

"That is Canada."

"Good to know in case I ever want to leave the country in a hurry."

"It is farther than it looks. Shall we go back?"

"Are you getting cold?"

"A little," she admitted.

They walked back to the house in silence. Bethany was overwhelmed by the smell of pine boughs when she entered the front door. The scent would always remind her of Michael in the future. She turned to face him. "Good night, Michael."

"You take care," he said as he went out into the night with Sadie Sue at his heels. Bethany sighed as she watched him walk up the hill. Being friends was truly the best path for them. Wasn't it?

Only the ache in her heart said it might not be enough.

Chapter Twelve

Bethany rose from bed feeling more rested than she had in weeks. Her first thought was to wonder if Michael shared the same feeling of relief that they were remaining friends, or did he hope for more one day?

She was fixing herself coffee when she heard a truck pull up in front of the house. She looked out the window. Mr. Meriwether got out of his delivery van and started for the house. The sheriff's SUV pulled up behind him. The look on their faces said it wasn't a social visit.

Bethany clutched her chest. "Oh, Ivan, what have you done now?"

Since he wasn't out of bed yet, he couldn't very well answer her question. She opened the door before Mr. Meriwether knocked. He inclined his head. "Good morning, Ms. Martin."

"Good day to you, Mr. Meriwether, Sheriff Lundeen. What can I do for you gentlemen?"

"I'm afraid we are here on an unpleasant errand," the sheriff said.

Mr. Meriwether nodded. "It sure is. Last night a little after midnight someone broke into one of my warehouses. They took several thousand dollars' worth of mechanic's tools, and brand-new toolboxes."

"What does that have to do with me?" she asked, fearing she knew the answer.

The sheriff removed his hat. "Is your brother, Ivan, at home?"

"*Ja*, he is here, though he is still abed."

The sheriff came in, forcing Bethany to step out of his way. "We're going to need to talk to him. The perpetrator was caught on a surveillance camera. It appears to be your brother arriving on foot and then he begins loading the stolen merchandise into a white panel van that pulled up just outside the fence. We didn't get a good look at the driver or the plates."

"It was an Amish boy fitting your brother's description," Mr. Meriwether added as he followed the sheriff inside.

Bethany led them into the living room with her heart pounding so hard she thought they must be able to hear it. This was serious. Thousands of dollars' worth of tools? This wasn't three chickens. She grew sick at heart. "I will go upstairs and get my brother. I'm sure he had nothing to do with this. Please have a seat."

"Thank you for your cooperation, ma'am." The sheriff sat on the edge of her sofa.

She hustled Ivan out of bed with only the briefest of explanations. She went into Jenny's room. "Jenny, get up and go get Michael. Tell him I need him right away."

"But I haven't had any breakfast."

"You can eat later. Now go."

The shock on Ivan's face when he saw the sheriff waiting for him told her he knew nothing about what was going on.

She stood beside Ivan. The sheriff began questioning him. Michael arrived twenty minutes later. "Can you fill me in?" he asked the law officer.

The sheriff looked him up and down. "Are you the boy's parent?"

"I'm not. I'm a friend."

"Then I don't see how this concerns you."

"I gave my word to our bishop that I would assume responsibility for Ivan's action. Anything that concerns him concerns me. If not, we must ask you to leave until the bishop and church elders can join us."

Bethany could see the wheels turning in the sheriff's mind. Did he want one Amish man or a whole roomful of them present for his questioning? Reluctantly he agreed to have Michael present and filled him in on what was known.

Michael was the one who picked up on a discrepancy. "You say the robbery took place a few minutes before eleven. We were here with Pastor Frank Pearson until ten thirty. We all saw Ivan go upstairs."

"But you admit that he could have left the premises after you did," the sheriff pointed out.

"You say a boy arrived on foot and a second perpetrator in a white panel van pulled up a few minutes later. Even if Ivan left here at 10:31, he would have been hard-pressed to run three miles in very cold temperatures and then calmly walk into Mr. Meriwether's warehouse and carry out the tools you claim were stolen."

Bethany could see the sheriff wavering. He said, "It's not outside the realm of possibility. He could have gotten a ride with the person in the van."

"But it is reasonable doubt," Michael insisted. "Were there fingerprints? Do you have a full view of his face on tape?"

Bethany was grateful for Michael's presence. He seemed to know exactly what to say.

The sheriff leaned forward on the couch and stared at Ivan. "We can't make a positive ID but it appears to be a boy wearing gloves, a dark coat and a black Amish hat."

Michael turned to Ivan. "Did you do it?"

Ivan shook his head. "*Nee.* I did not."

The sheriff sighed as he rose to his feet. "I don't have enough to hold the boy at this point. I have to wait for my forensics team to process the scene. Ivan, you can't leave town. Do you understand?"

Ivan nodded. Michael said, "Believe me, we want you to find this guy as much as you want to find him."

After the sheriff and Meriwether left, Bethany knelt in front of her brother and took his hand. "What do you know about this?"

"I think I can get the tools back, but I'm not going to turn anyone in."

"You can't protect Jeffrey forever," Michael said softly.

"You don't understand. I have to help him."

"Do you know who was driving the van?" Michael asked.

He shook his head. "I'm not sure."

Ivan left the room and Bethany didn't think twice about throwing herself into Michael's arms. She needed him. And he was there for her. "What should I do? I thought sending him to live with my uncle was terrible, but sending him to jail is unthinkable."

"It won't come to that. He's a juvenile. Besides, the evidence they have is circumstantial."

She leaned back to look at his face. "How do you know so much about police proceedings?"

"You know the store where I worked last year was robbed. I answered questions from the police for weeks on end. I can't believe I was able to listen to his interrogation without breaking down. I guess I really am doing better," he mumbled more to himself than to her.

She gazed at his dear face. "Thank you for everything."

He held her away and took a step back. "That's what friends do."

Early the following morning, Bethany heard a car turn into her drive. It was the sheriff again. Had he come to arrest Ivan? He stopped a few feet from her walkway and got out. She opened the door as he reached the porch with her heart in her throat. "Good morning, Sheriff."

"Good morning. Is Ivan here?"

"I hope so. I haven't seen him yet. Has there been another robbery?" She braced herself to hear the answer.

"No. In fact, just the opposite has occurred. Sometime during the night all the tools and equipment stolen from Mr. Meriwether's property were left outside his gate. There doesn't appear to be any damage. Nothing is missing. Mr. Meriwether is dropping all the charges."

Relief made her knees weak. "That's wonderful news." It wouldn't keep Ivan from being sent to live with Uncle Harvey, but it was so much better than having him go to jail that it didn't seem horrible anymore. She couldn't wait to tell Michael.

After the sheriff left, Bethany pulled on her coat and boots, intent on seeing Michael, but a knock on the door stopped her. She opened it and saw Mrs. Morgan, Jeffrey's mother, on the porch. The woman had a large bruise on her face and a split lip.

"Mrs. Morgan, what happened? Come in. Do you need to go to the hospital?" Bethany put her arm around the woman and helped her inside.

"Don't mind me. This is nothing. Is Jeffrey here? He didn't come home last night."

"He's not here. You must be out of your mind with worry. Let me get Ivan. Maybe he knows where Jeffrey is. Come in and sit down." The woman entered the kitchen and sat down as Bethany raced up the stairs to Ivan's room. She sagged with relief when she saw he was still in bed. She shook his shoulder. "Ivan, wake up. Mrs. Morgan is downstairs. She says Jeffrey is missing. Do you know where he is?"

Ivan sat up, rubbing his face. "I thought he was at home."

"When was the last time you saw him?"

"About midnight."

"Midnight? You went out last night?"

"Yeah. I'm sorry. I had to."

Bethany considered sending him to fetch Michael, but she realized there was nothing Michael could do. She went downstairs and found Mrs. Morgan with arms crossed and her head down on the kitchen table, weeping.

Bethany sat down beside her and put her arm around the woman's shoulders. "It's going to be all right. Ivan hasn't seen him since last night."

Michael appeared in the workshop doorway. "What's going on?"

Bethany quickly filled him in. He came and sat down across from Mrs. Morgan. "I think you should call the police."

Mrs. Morgan looked up and clutched Bethany's arm. "No. I can't do that."

Two nights later, Sadie's low growl brought Michael wide-awake. She left his bedside and trotted to the door. He sat up in bed. "What's wrong, girl?"

Sadie whined, looked back at him and whined again. Michael slipped out of bed, pulling the top quilt over himself against the cold night air. "I'm coming."

He made his way to the window beside the door. He used the corner of the quilt to wipe the frost from the center of the glass. He was expecting to see a lynx or coyote. Instead he watched a human figure approach the back door of Bethany's home and disappear into the shadows. His heart started pounding. Was she in danger?

He tossed the quilt aside, quickly pulling on his clothes and boots. He grabbed his coat from the hook by the door and pulled it on as he stepped outside. Sadie stood by his side but she wasn't growling. She looked at him. He nodded. "Go find him."

She started toward Bethany's house with Michael close behind her. The beam of a flashlight shone from the open back door. Michael couldn't see who was holding it, but he did see the person the light settled on. It was Jeffrey Morgan. The boy entered the house and the light went out. When the kitchen light came on, Michael decided to investigate further. Sadie was already at the back door, scratching and whining to be let in. Michael stood in the shadow of the pine tree off to the side and waited. When the door opened it was Ivan. "Sadie, stop it. You'll wake everybody. Go home."

Michael stepped out of the shadows. "Good evening, Ivan."

The boy's eyes widened in shock. "Michael. What are you doing here?"

"Sadie alerted me to a prowler. You've got some explaining to do."

"I reckon I do. Come into the kitchen." He turned and walked down the hall. Michael followed him.

Jeffrey was at the kitchen table, eating baked beans straight out of the can. As Michael watched Jeffrey tear into his food, it reminded him of the first time he saw Sadie gulp a sandwich down in one bite. Michael looked at Ivan. "What's going on?"

Jeffrey stopped eating to glance at Ivan and shook his head no.

Ivan spread his hands wide. "We can't do it by ourselves. Michael will help."

"He'll make me go back."

Michael took a seat across the table from Jeffrey. Ivan sat beside his friend. "Jeffrey can't go home. He isn't safe there."

Jeffrey had stopped eating and was staring down at the table. "I won't go back."

Michael reached across the table and put two fingers under the boy's chin. Jeffrey flinched but didn't pull away. Michael lifted the child's face until Jeffrey looked at him. "I know a lot about being afraid. I won't make you do anything that you don't want to do. Why don't you tell me about it?"

Jeffrey compressed his lips into a thin line. It was Ivan who spoke. "His dad beats him."

"He hits my mom, too," Jeffrey added in a small voice.

Michael sat back. He had suspected as much after Mrs. Morgan refused to call the police or go to the hospital, but this was beyond his ability to help. He wished Bethany was here.

Jeffrey stuck his fork in the empty can. "That's why I got so mad when I learned you were going to be staying in the cabin. I used to stay there when things are bad at home. I'm sorry I broke your window."

"I thought Ivan threw the rock." Michael glanced between the boys.

Jeffrey looked at Ivan. "He took the blame for me. He sticks up for me a lot."

"The stolen supplies from Jedidiah—was that your doing or Ivan's?"

The boys exchanged guilty glances. Ivan wrinkled his nose. "It was sort of my idea. The bishop preaches that we have to share with those in need. I figured Jedidiah would share if he knew, so I took what I thought he could spare. I didn't know he'd be so upset about it. I was going to leave him a note but I didn't have paper or a pen with me."

"He only did it to help my family. Sometimes my mom and my little brother and sister don't have enough to eat. I helped him carry the stuff," Jeffrey added. "We're sort of both to blame."

Michael sighed. "I see you are equal partners in crime, as it were."

The boys nodded.

Michael shook his head in disbelief. "It's always better to ask first. And the chickens?"

"Mom had to cook our laying hens a few weeks ago. The little ones missed having eggs in the morning. I only took what we needed to eat."

"How did you boys get the tools returned to Mr. Meriwether?"

Jeffrey looked pleased. "I sort of borrowed my dad's van. I know how to drive it. He hadn't sold the stuff yet." The boy's grin faded. "He got real mean when he found the stuff was missing. I had to get away."

Ivan locked his pleading gaze on Michael. "What are you going to do now? You can't make him go home."

Michael rubbed his aching leg, stalling for time. He didn't know what to do. If Jeffrey was a member of the Amish faith, he would take this to the bishop. This required someone with a level head and a compassionate heart. "Ivan, I think you should go wake your sister."

"I'm up." Bethany came into the room, pulling

the belt of her pink robe tight. "I overheard most of this conversation. Jeffrey, do you know your mother is worried sick about you?"

He shrugged one shoulder. "I left her a note tonight. She'll know I'm okay when she reads it."

Michael exchanged a knowing look with Bethany. She sat down beside him. He was glad of her presence. She smiled softly at Jeffrey. "You're a thirteen-year-old boy and it's winter in Maine. How are you surviving? Where are you staying?"

Jeffrey wouldn't look at her. "Here and there."

"And how often in the past two days have you had a decent meal?"

He lifted the empty can. "Tonight."

Michael shared a speaking glance with Bethany.

"What should we do?" she asked, speaking Pennsylvania Dutch. "He isn't Amish. The *Englisch* have many rules about children."

"They do have complicated laws about child custody. I know that much from my time in the outside world. We could be in trouble for not telling the police he is here."

Jeffrey surged to his feet. "I don't know what you're saying but I won't go back."

Michael held up one hand to reassure him. "We are not suggesting that. I think going to Pastor Frank is our best option. He will listen to you,

Jeffrey, and he will make the right decision. He will not put you in harm's way."

Jeffrey sank back onto his chair. Ivan laid a hand on his shoulder. "Pastor Frank is a good fellow. You can trust him."

Bethany leaned forward and took Jeffrey's hands in hers. "You have to trust us. We want what is best for both you and your mother. You can't stay out in this weather. You could die."

"That would be better than going back to him."

Michael stood up. "You and I are going to go see Pastor Frank and tell him the situation. I know he will do the right thing. You can try running away again, Jeffrey, but you will be easy to track in the snow. I don't think you'll get far."

Jeffrey put his head down on his folded arms and began to cry.

Bethany waited for Michael to return. She left a lamp on so he would know she was up. It was almost four thirty when he stepped through the door. He looked tired and he was limping heavily. She wanted to throw her arms around him and help him to the sofa but she wasn't sure he would appreciate that gesture. "How did it go?"

He sat down on the sofa beside her with a deep sigh. "Children are complicated creatures. I'm surprised parents choose to have more than one."

"That's a very cynical thing to say. Humans

are indeed complicated creatures. Since the good Lord made more than one of us, I assume He sees something wonderful in each of us."

"Even Mr. Morgan?"

"Even him. He deserves forgiveness and our prayers as much if not more than anyone."

Michael sighed. "I know you're right. That is what our faith teaches us. That is what our Lord commands us to do, but sometimes it is hard living by those words. That boy was covered with bruises."

"Pastor Frank didn't make Jeffrey go back to his father, did he?"

"He knew exactly what to do. He notified the police and reported the child abuse. Jeffrey and his brother and sister were taken to a children's home where they will be well cared for until permanent placement can be found. Frank is sure they'll go back to their mother when she is ready. Jeffrey's mother chose to go to a women's shelter."

"And Jeffrey's father?"

"Mr. Morgan was arrested and taken to jail. He is wanted in another state for burglary and arson. Apparently he often made Jeffrey steal stuff for him. It was his idea to dress Jeffrey in Amish clothing in case he was seen. Jeffrey said it was his father who damaged Greg Janson's tractor and let Robert Morris's cattle loose. He felt both men owed him more money for work he'd done for them last summer. It seems they fired him and hired two Amish fellows instead."

"At least everyone will know now that Ivan wasn't to blame for those things. I hope the bishop will reconsider letting him stay with me now. I'll speak to him tomorrow."

"Ivan still made some poor decisions but his heart was in the right place."

She reached out and covered Michael's hand with her own. His fingers were cold. "I was truly glad that you were here to help tonight. I have no idea what I would have done without your guidance."

A small smile lifted one corner of his lips. "You would have figured it out."

She shook her head. "I don't think so. When that little boy started crying at the table, I just wanted to wrap him in a warm blanket and carry him up to a soft bed. He broke my heart."

Michael laced his fingers with hers. "I know just what you mean. It was like finding Sadie all over again. Speaking of which, where is she?"

"Jenny had a nightmare about an hour ago. Sadie is sleeping with her."

He drew back a little. "You let a dog sleep in Jenny's bed? This from a woman who says dogs don't belong in the house?"

"I can admit when I am wrong. Sadie will always be welcome in my house. Provided she has had a bath and that she doesn't have fleas."

"I knew I was forgetting something."

"What?"

"Flea powder for her. Did you notice her scratching a lot?" He began scratching the back of his head.

Bethany popped him on the shoulder. "You are not as funny as you think you are."

He winked. "I'm funny enough to get a smile out of you."

As he gazed at her, his grin slowly faded. She sensed a change come over him. Her heart began beating heavily. He moved closer and she didn't pull away. He cupped her cheek with one hand, sending her pulse pounding and stealing her breath. She waited for his kiss. He caressed her lips with his thumb. "I should go."

She couldn't think clearly, let alone come up with a single objection.

He rose abruptly and left the house.

Chapter Thirteen

Bethany spoke to the bishop the next afternoon at his business. Michael wasn't with her. She relayed her brother's involvement and stressed his innocence. "He believed he was protecting Jeffrey from his father's foul temper. You have to respect him for trying to do good."

"I'm sympathetic to your position, Bethany, but I haven't changed my mind. Ivan followed too eagerly after this *Englisch* boy and he had made poor decisions. You can't deny that. I still feel the boy will benefit from a full-time male role model."

"Michael is providing Ivan with guidance. The two of them get along well and Ivan has improved so much." She held her breath, praying the bishop would see things her way.

"My mind is made up on this. The boy will benefit from his uncle's counsel evermore."

She pressed her hands together. "Please reconsider—"

He cut her off. "Bethany, go home and raise your sister. Your brother will return to you in time if it is God's will."

She had lost. Bethany left the bishop's workplace devoid of hope. If she wanted to keep her family together, the only thing left for her to do was to move away from New Covenant and start over somewhere else, but she had no idea where to go and no money to start over with.

The evening of the community Christmas play was chilly with overcast skies that promised more snow. Ivan insisted they use the sleigh to travel to the community building. He said it was more Amish and it felt more Christmas-like. Both children were excited because there would be a small gift exchange after the program that the bishop had agreed they could participate in.

Michael brought the sleigh to Bethany's front door and spread a thick lap robe over her when she got in. "I don't want you to catch cold."

"Ivan! Come on," Jenny shouted from the back seat, causing the patient horse to toss his head and snort. Ivan came out the door, letting it slam shut behind him. He had been trying to act as if the program was no big deal, but Michael could see he was excited, too. The teenager piled in the back seat with his sister.

After a second or two of getting settled, Ivan said, "Scoot over, Jenny, and give me some room."

"I'm cold and you have more of the blanket."

"I do not."

"You do so."

"Enough," Bethany said, putting an end to the rising family squabble.

Michael lifted his arm and laid it along the back of the seat to give Bethany more room. She moved closer. As much as he wanted to slip his arm around her shoulders, he knew it would be a bad idea. He was already having far too much trouble remembering to treat her as a friend.

"Ready, everyone?" Michael asked. Three confirmations rang out. He slapped the lines and the big horse took off down the snow-covered lane.

Sleigh bells jingled merrily in time to the horse's footfalls. The runners hissed along over the snow as big flakes began to float down. They stuck to Michael's and Ivan's hats, turning their brims white. Jenny tried to catch snowflakes on her tongue between giggles.

Michael leaned down to see Bethany's face. "Are you warm enough?" She nodded, but her cheeks looked rosy and cold. Michael took off his woolen scarf and wrapped it around her head to cover her mouth and nose.

"Danki," she murmured. "Won't you be cold?"

"Nope. It's a perfect evening, isn't it?" The snow obscured the mountains. The fields lay hidden beneath a thick blanket of white. Pine tree branches drooped beneath their icy loads. A hushed stillness filled the air, broken only by the jingle of the harness bells. It was a picture-perfect moment in time and Michael wished it could go on forever.

The community building was only a few miles from the farm in a converted brick factory not far from the city center. For Michael, they reached their destination much too quickly. As they drew closer they saw a dozen buggies and sleighs parked along the south side of the building out of the wind while the parking lot in front of it was full of cars and trucks.

As the kids scrambled out of the sleigh, Michael offered Bethany his hand to help her out. When she took it, he gave her an affectionate squeeze. She graced him with a shy smile in return.

Inside the building, the place was already crowded with people. What had once been the factory floor held rows of folding chairs facing a small stage at the front. Swags of fragrant cedar boughs graced the sills of the tall multipaned windows. A Christmas tree stood in one corner, decorated with colorful paper chains, popcorn and cranberry strands, and handmade ornaments made by the children. A table on the opposite wall bore trays of cookies and candies and a large punch bowl. An atmosphere of joy, goodwill and anticipation permeated the air.

Several *Englisch* people Michael didn't know approached Bethany to tell her how happy they were to learn Ivan had been cleared and how glad they were to have Amish neighbors. Everywhere Michael looked there were welcoming smiles. He had been prepared to feel uneasy in the crowd but he didn't. The Martin children hurried to join their classmates behind the stage. Michael and Bethany found seats out front a few minutes before the curtain rose.

The children performed their assigned roles, singing songs and reciting poetry. Then it came time for Jenny to narrate the Christmas story. She walked out on stage in her white robe with her long hair in two golden braids. Michael glanced at Bethany. Her eyes brimmed with maternal pride. He squeezed her hand and together they watched the community's children bring the story of the first Christmas to life.

When the play was over, Jenny held one hand high. "*Frehlicher Grischtdaag*, everyone. Merry Christmas!"

The curtain fell and Michael clapped until

his hands hurt. The last song of the evening was Ivan's solo. To Michael's surprise, the boy had a beautiful voice. His a cappella rendition of "O Come, O Come, Emmanuel" brought tears to a few eyes, including Bethany's.

Later, when everyone had a plate of treats, Jenny squeezed in between Bethany and Michael. He said, "You did well, Jenny. Your narration was very good."

"Danki."

Bethany slipped her arm around the child and gave her a hug.

Michael rubbed Ivan's head. "Who knew you could sing so well?"

The boy blushed with happiness. Everyone seemed happy, only Bethany's joy appeared forced.

It was full dark by the time the festivities wound down and families began leaving. Michael brushed the accumulated snow from the sleigh's seats and lit the lanterns on the sides. The horse stood quietly, one hip cocked and a dusting of snow across his back. Michael stepped back inside to tell Bethany they were ready.

Scanning the room, he saw her with a group of young Amish women. Two of them held babies on their hips. Bethany raised a hand to smooth the blond curls of a little boy. As she did, her gaze met Michael's across the room.

In that moment, he knew exactly what he wanted. He wanted Bethany to have the life she was meant to live and he wanted to be a part of it. He wanted to spend every Christmas with her for the rest of his life. If only he could be certain his PTSD wouldn't return.

"Is it time to go home? I'm tired." Jenny, sitting on the bottom bleachers, could barely keep her eyes open.

"Yes, it's time to go home." He picked her up and she draped herself over his shoulder. Bethany joined them a minute later. In the sleigh, Michael let Ivan take the reins while he settled in with Jenny across his lap and Bethany seated beside him. The snow had stopped. A bright three-quarter moon slipped in and out of the clouds as they made their way home.

Snuggled beneath a blanket with Bethany at his side, Michael marveled at the beauty of the winter night in the far north and at the beauty of the woman next to him. When they pulled up in front of her house, Michael carried Jenny inside and up to bed while Ivan took the horse to the barn.

Michael stepped back as Bethany tucked her sister in. "I had a wonderful time. Thank you for inviting me."

"I'm glad." She closed the door to Jenny's room and faced him in the hall.

He stepped closer. She didn't move away.

Reaching out, he cupped her cheek. "Good night, Bethany."

"Good night, Michael." Her voice was a soft whisper. Slowly, he lowered his lips to hers and kissed her.

Bethany melted into Michael's embrace. His kiss was gentle and so very sweet. Their mutual decision to take a step back and simply remain friends vanished from her thoughts as she slipped her arms around his neck. He briefly pulled her closer, and then he let her go and took a step away. "I'll see you tomorrow."

She pressed a hand to her lips to hold on to that wondrous moment. Ivan came walking up the stairs and passed them on the way to his room. Embarrassed, Bethany wondered if he had seen her in Michael's arms. He muttered a polite good-night and went in his room. Maybe he hadn't seen anything.

She mumbled a quick goodbye to Michael and fled into her room. She closed the door and leaned against it. There was no way they could go back to being just friends now.

Could she accept him without knowing the secret part of his past he wouldn't share? His kiss seemed to indicate he wanted to be a part of her life, but he hadn't said anything about what kind of future he saw and if she had a place in it.

Christmas was less than two weeks away, and she was going to lose her brother if she failed to convince the bishop to change his mind. Was Gemma right? Was Michael the answer to her prayers?

Chapter Fourteen

Sadie rose from her spot beside the fireplace the next morning and trotted to the front door, wagging her tail. She looked back at Michael and whined. A second later he heard a timid knock. He sprang out of his chair, hoping it was Bethany, and twisted his bad leg in the process. There was so much he wanted to say to her.

He pulled open the door. Jenny, not Bethany, stood on his stoop. She was dressed in a dark blue snowsuit and coat with bright red mittens on her hands. The ribbons of her *kapp* dangled out from beneath her hood. Behind her stood four other bundled-up children. Two boys wore flat-topped black hats, so he knew they were Amish *kinder*. They were all pulling colorful plastic toboggans.

Jenny grinned eagerly. "Can Sadie come out and play with us?"

He glanced down at the dog standing beside

him. She wiggled with excitement but she didn't dash out the door. She looked to him for instructions. "I reckon."

He held the door wider and tipped his head toward the outside. "Go on. Have some fun."

Sadie bounded out of the house, jumping in circles around the children and barking.

"*Danki*, Michael," Jenny shouted as they headed toward his barn. He noticed that she was pulling two sleds, one red and one yellow. Why two? Every other child had one. Perhaps they were meeting someone else. They'd only gone a few more feet when he saw Jenny give the rope of one sled to Sadie. She held it in her mouth and trotted along with the group.

They disappeared behind the barn where the ground dropped away sharply, making a perfect hill for sledding. Although he couldn't see them, he could hear them calling encouragement to Sadie. The day was warmer than the past two weeks had been. He glanced back at the business paperwork waiting for him and decided it was time for a break.

He grabbed his hat and coat, put them on and closed the cabin door behind him. A walk in the fresh air was exactly what he needed. Maybe he would walk down and see Bethany. He smiled at the memory of their kiss last night. He was head over heels for her and he believed she felt the same but they hadn't discussed their feelings.

Maybe he was reading more into a kiss than he should. Bethany didn't know about his PTSD. Would that change her feelings toward him? He was better, it had been almost a month since he'd had a flashback, but was he well enough to consider a future with her? How would he know when he was healed?

A freshly shoveled path led from his cabin to Bethany's house. Ivan kept it open for him when he came to chop wood. That was the direction Michael wanted to go but he didn't have an excuse to see Bethany. He didn't want to appear too eager or pushy. The tracks of the children and dog led the other way.

He followed along, trying not to slip and fall in the new snow. When he reached the edge of the barn, he had an excellent view of the children sledding down the hill. Sadie was at the bottom with Jenny. They began to trudge back up, taking care to avoid the others flying down the hill toward them. Jenny was pulling her sled while Sadie pulled the other up the incline. He had never seen a dog do that.

At the top of the hill Jenny positioned her sled, sat down and pushed off with her hands. To his amazement, Sadie jumped on her own sled and went flying down the hill with her ears fluttering backward.

"Michael?"

He turned at the sound of Bethany's voice and saw her walking toward him. She held a package under her arm. He beckoned her closer. "You have to see this."

She smiled as she approached him. "This came for you in the mail. I thought it might be important and you weren't in your workshop."

"I was catching up on some paperwork. You need to see what the children are up to. Jenny stopped by to ask if Sadie could come out and play."

Bethany giggled. He would never tire of hearing her mirth. It always made him smile. He stepped to the side so that she could have his vantage point. He stumbled and would have fallen if she hadn't grabbed his coat to steady him. It was a good reminder that he wasn't fit. Sometimes he forgot how damaged he was when she was around.

She didn't say anything but set his package on a stone by the barn door. She stepped to where he had been standing and looked at the children. "Your dog is sledding all by herself. Did you teach her to do that?"

The wonder and amusement in her voice

eased the embarrassment he felt. "*Nee*, this is the first time."

"Oh, she's pulling it back up the hill. I don't believe it. It's like she's one of the children. That is a remarkable animal."

And you are a remarkable woman. For a second he was afraid he had spoken aloud.

"What are you two looking at?" Ivan asked as he walked up beside them. Jeffrey was with him. The boy, his younger siblings and his mother had returned to their home a few days after his father's arrest.

"We are watching Sadie use a sled," Bethany said.

"Are you fooling me?" Ivan walked to the edge of the slope and Jeffrey followed him. They began packing the snow into a ball and rolling it around to make it bigger. When they had one about a foot in diameter they pushed it down the hill toward the group of children.

"Not a good idea." Michael shouted, "Look out below!"

The snowball quickly gained size and speed. Both boys sprinted after it as did Bethany. Michael watched helplessly, knowing he wouldn't be of any use.

Sadie barked and raced up the hill to meet the ball. She leaped to the side and tried to bite it as it rolled past. Her actions changed the direction just enough to let it roll harmlessly past the little girl who fell trying to scramble out of the way.

The snowball came to rest a few feet away from the trees that separated the field from the road. Michael heard Ivan apologizing. "I didn't think it would get so big. I thought it would break apart."

Bethany eyed him sternly.

"Honest, sister. I wasn't trying to hurt anyone. I thought we could make a snowman faster by rolling the balls down the hill to make them bigger."

She looked up at Michael as if seeking his opinion. He didn't think the boys meant any harm, either. He nodded slightly. She turned back to her brother. "Okay. It was almost a good idea. It just shows that you have to consider all parts of a problem before you decide on a solution. The easy way is not often the best way."

The younger children eagerly began creating snowmen of their own.

Jenny beckoned to Michael. "Help me make a tall snowman, Michael."

He wanted to join them. How many happy memories would it take to make him forget the horrible ones? Even if he wanted to, there was no way he could get down the hill without falling and arriving at the bottom inside a massive snowball. He shook his head and held up his cane.

Jenny pulled her sled over to Sadie and whispered something in her ear. Then she gave her the rope. Sadie came charging up the hill, pulling the empty sled. She skidded to a stop in front of Michael, dropped the rope and began barking furiously.

He looked at his dog. "You can't be serious. You want me to sled down the hill." He took another look at the terrain. It actually wasn't a bad idea. He looked at all the people beckoning him to come down. Getting down was the easy part. Getting up the slope would be the real challenge.

Sadie jumped up and put her paws on his chest. He ruffled her ears. "What kind of Amish man gives in to the whims of children and dogs?"

She barked once and looked downhill.

He followed her gaze and saw Bethany watching him. "Good point. She is down there. I was looking for an excuse to spend some time with her. When an opportunity falls into my lap I shouldn't waste it."

He awkwardly lowered himself into the red plastic sled and used his cane to pull himself to the edge of the incline. He looked at Sadie. "If I break my other leg I'm going to blame you." He pushed off and went flying down the slope.

He remembered how much fun it was to go sledding down a hill when he was a child. As an adult, he was a little more concerned about arriving at his destination in one piece.

* * *

Bethany held her breath as Michael shot down the hill with more speed than any of the children had obtained. To her relief, he used his cane as a drag to slow down when he neared the bottom. He came to rest a few feet in front of her. All the children applauded. Ivan jumped forward to help him to his feet. Michael was laughing like one of the *kinder*.

She had never seen him so lighthearted. It seemed that whatever had plagued him when he first came to New Covenant was giving way to a happier man.

She turned around with a snowball in her hand. "I've been wanting to do this for quite some time." She threw the ball and it hit him in the chest.

He brushed at his coat. "I refuse to get in a snowball fight with you. It's not dignified."

"You're right." She scooped up another handful of snow and packed it together. "I wouldn't want you to do something undignified." She let fly and this one struck him on his shoulder.

He brushed the loose snow away with one hand. "You are asking for trouble."

"I don't think so. I'm pretty sure I can outrun you."

"That was a low blow."

She tossed a newly formed snowball from

one hand to the other. "You said you didn't like being treated differently because you need to use a cane."

"I think I will have to make you pay for that remark." He advanced menacingly.

She scuttled backward. "Forgiveness is the foundation of our religion. You don't want me to tell the bishop that you threatened me, do you?"

He kept coming and she kept backing up. "I think he would understand," he growled.

She took another step and tripped over the snowball Jenny had left unfinished. Michael scooped up a handful of snow. Standing over her, he dumped it on her face. She shrieked and rolled away. Surging to her feet, she shook her head to get rid of the snow and then glared at him. "That was just plain mean."

She was adorable. Her cheeks were bright red from the cold. Snow sparkled on her hair and eyelashes. The joy that filled his heart caught him off guard. Meeting her was the best thing that ever happened to him. How had she managed to worm her way so firmly into his heart in such a short amount of time?

"I apologize. I promise no more snow in the face, but I must remind you that you started it."

She looked as if she wanted to argue but gave in. "Okay, that is true. Now I have had my comeuppance and we are even, right?"

"I'd say so."

The boys had managed a haphazard snowman with a ragged straw hat, but they decided to go on to other adventures, leaving the slightly crooked fellow leaning into the wind.

"He looks lonely," Bethany said.

Michael put his hands on his hips. "I think he just looks homely."

Bethany moved several paces back. "I've been told I need to look at the whole picture."

"And what do you see?"

"A homely, lonely snowman. Let's fancy him up."

They found some winterberry and holly to decorate his straw hat. Bethany used a handful of red berries pressed into the snow to form his mouth. Michael supplied the branches for his arms and he sent one of the children to get a carrot for his nose.

Bethany withdrew a pace to look at him when he was finished. "There's still something missing."

"What?"

"I know." She pulled the red-and-white-striped scarf off and wrapped it around the snowman's neck. "There. He looks great."

Michael chuckled. "He looks like a mighty fancy Amish fellow. Is he one of your suitors?"

"He is and I will accept his offer." It was now

or never. She smoothed the snowman's rough cheeks with her mittens, knowing Michael was listening. She'd never been so bold in her life, but she had to try. "The bishop understands why Ivan acted as he did when I explained things to him the other day, but he is still convinced a firmer hand could have prevented much of the trouble Ivan became embroiled in. He won't reconsider sending my brother away. I need an Amish husband before Christmas and the Lord has provided. That is, unless another suitor speaks up and asks me for my hand in marriage." She couldn't look at Michael.

He stepped close to her. "I don't think you should marry this fellow."

She looked into Michael's troubled eyes. "Do you think I'll get a better offer?"

He shook his head and walked away from her. "I wish I could be the man you need, but I'm not, Bethany."

"I think you are."

"You make it so hard to say no."

She moved to stand in front of him. "If it's hard to say no, then maybe you should say yes. I won't make any demands on you. Your time will be your own. You can have one hundred percent of the business. I need your help, Michael."

"I'm sorry."

Jenny came walking back to see what they

were up to. She clapped her hands when she saw the snowman. "He's beautiful. He can be Bishop Schultz come to marry Michael and Bethany." Jenny looked at her sister.

Bethany gave Michael a sidelong glance. His face could have been carved from stone. She leaned over and forced a smile for her little sister. "There isn't going to be a wedding. I told you that."

Jenny's face fell. "Okay. I'm going to help Jeffrey and Ivan build a snow cave."

Michael glanced at Bethany and then quickly looked down at his boots. "Are you going to the Christmas parade in the city with Pastor Frank?"

"Yes, we are. What about you?" She avoided meeting his gaze.

"I think I will go." Maybe during the Christmas parade would be a good time to gauge how she felt about them.

Bethany retreated a pace. "I'd better get started on lunch. They're going to be a hungry bunch when they come in."

"I've got some work to do, too."

She regained some of her composure. "That's right. A box came for you. I left it at your barn."

He looked up the slope. "I might work on something that's already in the workshop."

"I'll get the box." She grabbed the empty toboggan that Jenny had left by her snowman's head and trudged up the hill. She picked up his box, got in the sled and pushed off.

When she came to a stop two feet in front of him, he arched one eyebrow. "Show-off."

"I'm just using the gifts God gave me." She handed him the box and walked beside him all the way to his workshop, but the awkwardness between them persisted. Had she ruined their friendship with her desperate attempt to keep Ivan?

A half hour later Bethany was at the kitchen sink, peeling potatoes for French fries, when Jeffrey came in. "I'm hungry. Can I have a sandwich?" Sadie Sue followed him in and plopped down in front of the fireplace with her tongue hanging out.

His cheeks were rosy red from the cold but his lips were tinged with blue. "I think you should stay in for a while. Take off your boots and let me check your feet."

She had learned her first winter here that frostbite was nothing to be trifled with. He did as she instructed. His toes were bright pink but there was a patch of white skin on the back of his left heel. "You are definitely not going back outside. I'm going to get a pan of cool water and I want you to keep your foot in it until I tell you otherwise."

"But we just finished a great snow cave. Ivan is expecting me to come back."

"I'll explain to him why you have to stay in."

Michael had been working in his shop but apparently he had overheard her conversation. "I'll go tell Ivan what's going on."

"Danki," Bethany said and smiled at him. He was always willing to lend a helping hand. In many ways he reminded her of her grandfather. He had the same kind of gentle soul. She fixed a pan of water and had Jeffrey soak his foot.

Michael put on his coat and hat. "Where is your snow cave?"

"Out by the highway. The snowplows have made huge piles there." The snow the previous night had left four more inches on the roadways.

Michael stepped out onto the porch. "I see the piles, but I don't see the kids."

Bethany came out and stood beside him. She shaded her eyes with one hand against the glare of the sun off the white snow. "I don't see them, either."

Mike took a pair of snowshoes off their hooks on the porch. As he did, Bethany heard the grading rumble of the snowplow coming down from the ridge. The truck with a large blade on the front blasted through the new snow, easily making bigger drifts along the side of the road. It was headed down to the intersection where Jeffrey said Ivan and Jenny were playing.

The snowplow driver couldn't see the children for they were on the far side of the high snowbank away from him. She saw a flash of red in the snow and thought it must be Jenny's glove. The snowplow hit the side of the big pile and pushed it farther off the edge of the highway, adding a huge new supply of snow on top of what was already there. The place where she had seen Jenny's glove was completely covered. She started screaming and ran toward her sister.

Michael saw the whole thing happen and was helpless to stop it. How much time did they have? A few minutes? Maybe more if the children were in any kind of air pocket. He turned around and hurried to the house. "Jeffrey, get your shoes back on and run to the neighbors. Jenny and Ivan have been buried by the snowplow. We need everybody who can get here to dig. Go."

Jeffrey rushed to do as he was told. Michael ran to the tower of snow. Bethany was on her knees, digging with her bare hands. Michael grabbed a snow shovel from the porch and rushed to her side. He gave it to her and began using his cane as a probe into the snow, hoping to come in contact with a body. Each time his cane sank all the way in, he prayed harder.

It seemed like hours but it could've only been

minutes when he heard the sounds of shouting from up the road. A dozen Amish men came rushing toward them with shovels and rakes. They spread out on either side of Bethany and Michael and began digging. Jeffrey was digging frantically with them. Bethany was crying. She kept saying "no, no, no."

He kept probing inch by inch, knowing Jenny and Ivan were under there somewhere and running out of time. He had never been so scared in his life. Not even when he knew the gunman was going to kill him. Suddenly Sadie Sue was beside him, whining. Bethany stopped digging and looked at the dog and then at Michael.

"It's a long shot," he said. He knelt beside Sadie and said, "Find Jenny." She whined and didn't move. Bethany came to stand beside Michael. "Find Jenny, please."

The dog trotted away from where they were digging and Michael's hopes crashed. He went back to probing and Bethany returned to digging.

Twenty feet away, Sadie Sue started barking and digging at the snow.

Bethany looked at Michael. "I saw her glove here. I know I did." She kept digging and uncovered a red plastic candy wrapper.

Jeffrey had returned. He took Bethany's shovel away and raced over to the dog. He began frantically scooping the snow aside as she dug her way in. Suddenly the dog disappeared completely.

Bethany heard crying and knew at least one of them was alive. Praying as she had never prayed before, she stumbled to where Jeffrey was kneeling. The rest of their neighbors gathered around the hole and began widening it. Sadie came backing out, but she was dragging something. With two strong tugs she emerged from the hole, pulling Jenny out by her coat. Ivan crawled out on his own.

Cheering broke out from everyone. Bethany grabbed up her sister and held her tight and threw her other arm around Ivan. "Thank you, merciful Lord."

She looked at Michael and held out her hand. He came and embraced them all. He never wanted to let them go. As his frantically beating heart slowed, he added Sadie Sue to the group hug. She started licking Jenny's face, making the child giggle.

Ivan looked at Michael. "I knew you'd find us."

Not once during the emergency had Michael thought about the robbery or its aftermath. He had faced a life-and-death challenge without triggering a flashback or a panic attack. He had worked side by side with Bethany to save her family. A family he wanted to be a part of forever.

He caught Bethany's eye. "If you haven't said yes to the snowman, I'd like to reconsider your offer."

"You would?" Hope brightened her face.

"I would."

"Is that a yes?" A grin spread across her face.

"If you'll have me."

"I will." She hugged Ivan and Jenny harder. "I most certainly will."

Chapter Fifteen

On the Saturday evening before Christmas, Bethany, Michael and the children climbed into Pastor Frank's twenty-passenger van with sixteen other members of their Amish community, including the bishop, Jesse, Gemma and her parents.

Bethany kept Jenny close to her. The child had been subdued since the accident and wanted to constantly claim Bethany's attention. Michael didn't seem to mind. Bethany loved him for that. Ivan seemed far less affected.

As the van rolled down the highway Ivan began leading them in song. Michael joined in with his pleasant baritone voice. Christmas hymns new and old filled Bethany's heart with the joy of this most holy season. She knew how blessed she was to have Jenny and Ivan with her and how easily it could have turned out differently. Every time she caught Michael's eye he smiled at her. She hoped it was just a matter of time before he declared his love.

When they reached the city Pastor Frank parked the van on a side street and everyone made their way to the parade route. The streets were lined four deep with bundled-up people all sharing the holiday spirit on a frosty evening. Lavish holiday lights decorated the buildings along Main Street, blinking red and green and ice blue. Lit displays filled every business window.

Jenny, standing at Bethany's side, tugged on her coat. "I can't see."

Jesse leaned down to her. "Would you like to sit on my shoulders? I can see everything and you'll be even taller."

Jenny glanced at Bethany and then took Jesse's hand. "Okay."

He hoisted her to sit piggyback on his shoulders and she laughed. "Ivan, look at me."

"Hey, that's not fair," her brother shot back, but he was smiling.

Bethany reached for Michael's hand and gave it a squeeze. "She's feeling better."

"Kids are resilient and there is nothing like seeing a parade from the back of a giant to perk someone up."

Bethany chuckled and leaned against him. "You can always make me laugh."

Michael knew a depth of joy he never thought he would experience. His PTSD had improved enough for him to believe he was finally over it. The stress of searching for Jenny and Ivan hadn't triggered a flashback. He hadn't even had a nightmare afterward. That horrible part of his life was well and truly over. He smiled at Bethany and took her hand. Although she hadn't said that she loved him, he was sure that love would blossom in time to match his. And he did love her. With all his heart.

A PA system announced the parade was about to start and the crowd pressed forward. The canon across the park boomed and fireworks lit up the sky. The red streaks in the darkness held his attention. A shiver crawled down his spine. He couldn't shake the sight of red streaks on the floor and red flashes lighting up the night beyond his window.

Sirens sounded. People cheered as the local police and firefighters led the parade in their new machines with lights and sirens. The crowd behind him pressed closer. Michael couldn't breathe. He started hearing a scream and knew it was coming from him. He couldn't shut out the screams. Someone was talking to him, asking him what was wrong. A hand grabbed him and he swatted it. He had to get away.

He felt the impact of the bullet hitting his leg. He fell to the ground and started moaning.

Bethany had no idea what was wrong with Michael. She cried out for help as she knelt beside him. People gathered round, pressing closer, staring, uncertain how to help. Michael gazed wide-eyed into the space, hitting at her when she touched him. Bethany didn't think he knew she was there. Suddenly Pastor Frank was beside her.

"It's okay, Michael. It's Pastor Frank. You're having a flashback. It isn't real. You aren't in any danger. You're safe. Can you hear me? Bethany is here beside me. Is it all right if Bethany holds your hand?"

Michael's hand opened and closed on the sidewalk. Bethany took hold of it. "It's all right, darling. I'm here. I'm with you."

Pastor Frank patted her shoulder. "Keep talking to him. He needs to know that what he is seeing and hearing isn't real. I think we're going to need to get him away from this noise and commotion. I'm going to bring the van up."

Pastor Frank summoned a police officer who went with him.

Bethany held Michael's hand but he kept moaning and muttering people's names. She had no idea how to help him. She'd never felt more useless in her life. She didn't understand what was wrong. Was this what he was afraid of? Jenny was on her knees beside Bethany, crying. "What's the matter with Michael?"

Ivan took his little sister by the shoulders. "He's going to be okay. He'll get over this soon."

Bethany prayed Ivan's words were true.

Michael refused to come out of his cabin the next day. He didn't want to see anyone. He didn't answer the door although he knew both Frank and Bethany were outside. What was the point? Everyone knew now that he was just a shell of a man who looked normal but wasn't. Pastor Frank had been right. He wasn't going to be able to heal himself. He needed help. If he had tried to get help earlier maybe he could've salvaged something of his relationship with Bethany.

When the sun started to set, he went out and harnessed the pony. Pastor Frank's survivors' support group was tonight. Michael wasn't sure he was a survivor, but he definitely needed support.

At the church, he left his horse and cart and walked around the back of the building. A set of steps led to the basement. The door of the room where support group meetings were held stood open. A hand-lettered sign on the wall said Welcome to a Safe Place.

He wasn't sure what a safe place felt like anymore but if he was ever going to find one he had to start somewhere. He stepped inside and stopped in surprise. There were eight *Englisch* men and women seated at a round table with the pastor, but there were a dozen chairs lined up across the back of the room filled with the men and women of his Amish community. Jesse and the bishop. The carpenter Nigel Miller and his wife, Becca. Gemma Lapp and her parents, plus a dozen other Amish people he didn't know by name.

Bethany rose from her seat and came toward him. She held out her hand but he didn't take it. "What are you doing here?"

"I'm here to learn about PTSD and how to help the man I love cope with and overcome this disorder. We all want to be able to help you when you need us."

"The man you love? How can you still say that after what you saw? I was on the pavement, sobbing like a frightened child. I wasn't even aware that you were beside me. How can you love someone who is so damaged? 'The man that you pity' is what you really mean to say. You pity me."

"How can I not love you? In all the world you are the man who opened my heart so that I could clearly see God has chosen you to be my beloved. Are you a perfect man? *Nee*, for only God is perfect. Are you a good man? I believe, I know that you are."

Michael tried to swallow the lump in his throat as tears stung his eyes. "I don't deserve your love."

She smiled at him softly. "I have news for you. God and I believe you do."

Pastor Frank came to stand beside Bethany. "I am delighted that you came tonight, Michael. I wasn't sure that you would, but all of your friends have expressed a sincere interest in learning about PTSD and about how to deal with someone who suffers from it."

Michael started backing away. "I can't do this. Not yet. Not here. I'm sorry, Bethany."

"Michael, please." She held out her hand.

"*Nee*, whatever you thought was between us is over. I'm no good to you." He turned and walked out the door.

Bethany watched helplessly as Michael turned his back on her and left. She didn't understand why he wouldn't even try to accept their help. She looked to Pastor Frank. "What do I do?"

"That's why you're here. To learn about what you can do."

"Should I go after him?"

"No. I'm going to ask everyone to have a seat

and I'm going to talk a little about PTSD and what it means to a person suffering from that disorder."

Bethany returned to her seat. Gemma grasped her hand.

Frank smiled at the crowd. "Some of you know exactly what I'm talking about. Others are just learning about the existence of this cruel disorder. Someone with PTSD will experience horrible events over and over again in a way that is so real they believe they are back in that situation."

Bethany listened and tried to learn all she could, but the magnitude of the problem was daunting. After the meeting was over she stayed to talk to Frank alone.

"Tell me how I can help Michael. Why did he push me away? I believe he loves me. I know he does."

"Michael considers himself weak. He is fearful that others, that you, will see him that way, too. Yet he can't hide from what has happened to him. He has tried to run away from it by moving to this remote settlement, but the change of scenery hasn't changed the disorder. But there is help and there is hope. I believe that shining God's light into the dark recesses of our pain will take away the power the trauma has over us."

"What do I do now?"

"When someone you love suffers from post-traumatic stress disorder, it can be overwhelming. You may feel hurt by your loved one's distance and moodiness. However, it's important to know that you're not a helpless bystander. Your love and support can make all the difference in Michael's recovery. Don't try to pressure him into talking. It may make things worse. Just let him know you're willing to listen when he wants to talk."

"I'm frightened. I'm not sure what I'm walking into but I love him. I have to help."

Michael had to leave. He couldn't stay and see the woman he loved look at him with pity for the rest of his life. He couldn't do it. He didn't own much. Just a few tools, some clothes and a big yellow dog. It should be easy to pick up and go, except it wasn't easy.

He was in the workshop, carefully packing up his tools, when the door opened. He knew who it was without looking. His eyes filled with tears but he refused to let them fall.

She spoke softly. "Please don't leave us."

"You must be out of your mind to want me to stay."

She stepped closer. "I don't think so. I think you're the man I need. You also happen to be the man I love."

His gaze flew to hers. "You don't know what you're saying."

"I know exactly what I'm saying. I am in love with you, Michael Shetler. My heart tells me you are the man I have been waiting for all my life."

He turned away and continued packing his tools. "You want a man who can fall apart in the blink of an eye because some sound or smell triggers a flashback? Is that your idea of an ideal mate? What if I'm driving a team and the children are with me and I don't see the train coming when I cross the tracks?"

"Michael, I know your problem looms large to you, but for me it is only one part of who you are. You are a kind, loving man. You are hardworking. You try to live your faith by caring for those around you. You are great with children and with dogs. You walk with a cane and you have PTSD. I won't pretend to understand what that is like for you. But do you really want to give up a woman who loves you, two children who adore you, and a mangy mutt that thinks you hung the moon?"

He put down his screwdrivers. "Sadie Sue isn't a mangy mutt."

"You're right. She is a very special gift sent by God to help us. She saved Ivan's and Jenny's lives, but I would trade places with that dog in a heartbeat. Do you know why? Because you accept that she loves you regardless of the difficulties you face. I wish you had half that much faith in my love. If you don't, then maybe I am wasting my breath."

* * *

Michael wanted to deny his love for Bethany but he couldn't. He knew it took a great deal of courage for her to come to him this way. She was the most remarkable woman he'd ever met.

"Bethany, I don't want to burden you with my weakness. You deserve a strong and stable man."

"I do." She gave him a sly smile. "Unfortunately, Jesse won't have me. That leaves you."

He grinned in spite of himself. "Jesse wouldn't stand a chance against your wit."

"You once told me that you would help me with anything I needed if it was within your power. Did you mean that?"

"I did."

"Then here is what I want. I want to be the person beside you the next time you have a flashback if you ever have one again. I want to know and understand what you are going through, what you are seeing and hearing so I can lead you to a safe place. Tell me what happened to you. Make me understand."

Michael shook his head. "I will never do that to you."

Her eyes filled with disappointment. "Why won't you let me help you?"

"You don't understand."

"Make me."

He stepped close and took her hands in his.

"Bethany, if I share with you the pain and guilt and the horrible events that I lived through, then they can become your nightmare, too. You will be haunted by the things I tell you because you love me. I don't want you to know even a small part of the horror I endured."

"I'm a strong woman."

"I know you are."

"Frank told me he suffered with PTSD for many years after he came back from his military service. It destroyed his marriage and almost took his life. He found a way to deal with it by helping others. He also told me that talking about what happened to you is a way to decrease the power it has over your mind."

"He may be right. I will share my story with him but not with you."

"Don't you trust me?"

"I trust you with my life and all that I have. You must trust me when I say there are some things you are better off not knowing."

"I guess you are asking me for a leap of faith. Okay. I will not ask about it again. Are you going to marry me?"

He shook his head in bewilderment. "You are too bold to be a *goot* Amish maiden."

"I'm an Amish maiden who knows what she wants. You think that marrying me will ruin my life. I'm going to tell you that the only way you can ruin my life is to not marry me. Don't break my heart."

She stepped closer and slid her arms around his neck. "Please, Michael, say that you love me or don't say it—because it doesn't matter. I already know you do. I see it in your eyes. I feel it in your touch. I know it by the way your heart calls to mine."

He groaned and wrapped his arms around her to pull her close. "I can't believe I'm about to give you the opportunity to tell me what to do for the rest of my life."

Michael leaned close. Bethany knew he was going to kiss her. She had never wanted anything more. His lips touched hers with incredible gentleness, a featherlight touch. It wasn't enough.

She cupped his face with her hands. To her delight, he deepened the kiss. Joy clutched her heart and stole her breath. She'd been waiting a lifetime for this moment and never knew it.

He pulled her closer. The sweet softness of his lips moved away from her mouth. He kissed her cheek, her eyelids and her forehead, and then he drew away. Bethany wasn't ready to let him go. She would never be ready to let him go.

"I love you, Bethany," he murmured softly against her temple. "You make me whole. I am broken but you believe I can be mended. You make me believe it. I have lived in despair, ashamed of what I don't understand. I thought I was beyond help. And then you came into my life and I saw hope."

"I love you, too, darling, but it is God that has made us both whole. Will you marry me?"

"To keep Ivan with you?" he asked.

She rose on tiptoe and kissed him. "To keep you by my side always. Will you?"

"Can't you hear my heart shouting the answer?" He kissed her temple and held her close.

Bethany had never felt so cherished. The wonder of his love was almost impossible to comprehend. Emotion choked her. She couldn't speak.

"Did he say yes?" Jenny's whispered question was hushed by Ivan.

Michael choked on a laugh as he realized they weren't alone. He looked up at the ceiling to compose himself. Bethany shook silently in his arms. He knew she was trying not to laugh out loud.

He mustered his most authoritative voice. "Eavesdroppers are likely to be sent to bed without their supper for a week."

Jenny popped up from behind the desk. "I wasn't eavesdropping. I just came in to ask my sister a question."

Michael kept his arm around Bethany as she

turned to face her sister. "Ivan, what is your excuse?" she asked.

Ivan rose more reluctantly. "I came in to keep Jenny from interrupting the two of you."

"And what is the reason the two of you were hiding behind my desk?" he asked.

"I wasn't hiding. I was scratching Sadie's tummy," Jenny announced with a smile at her brilliant excuse. "But I did happen to hear my sister ask you to marry her, Michael. I thought men were supposed to ask first. Did she do it backward?"

Ivan took her hand and started to lead her from the room. "You have a lot to learn, sis. Women like to let men think it was their idea."

Jenny tried to get her hand loose. "Wait. We didn't hear his answer." Ivan didn't let go of her. She grabbed the doorjamb and held on as she looked over her shoulder. "Please, Michael, say you want to marry us."

A tug from her brother propelled her out of the room. He shut the door with a resounding bang.

Bethany turned and leaned against Michael's chest as she shook with laughter. "I'm the one who should tell you to run and get as far away from us as fast as you can."

"I'm afraid that no matter how far I went I wouldn't survive long."

She leaned back to look at his face. "Why is that?"

"Because my heart would remain here in your keeping and a man can't live long without a heart."

"Then you will marry me?" she asked hopefully.

"On one condition."

A faint frown appeared on her face. "What condition?"

"That I also get to ask the question. Bethany Martin, will you do me the honor of becoming my wife?"

"I will."

"Then I promise to love and cherish you all the days of my life," he said and bent to kiss her once more.

The door flew open and Jenny charged in with Sadie at her side. "He said yes and she said yes. We're getting married!" Sadie started barking wildly as she bounced around Jenny. Ivan stood in the doorway with a bright smile on his face.

Bethany gazed up at Michael with all the love in her heart. "Are you sure you want to marry all of us?"

He kissed the tip of her nose. "I want an Amish wife for Christmas, two fine Amish children, a fine house with a workshop and a *goot hund*. What more could a man need?"

"Maybe another kiss from his Amish wife?"

"My darling Bethany, you read me like a book." He leaned in and kissed her again, knowing no matter what trials he faced, he would never face them alone. God and Bethany would be with him always.

Chapter Sixteen

The morning of Second Christmas, December 26, dawned clear and bright in New Covenant, Maine. Bethany and Michael stood in the entryway of her house and greeted their wedding guests. Bethany's aunt and uncle had arrived on Christmas Eve and had helped take over the preparations for the wedding. Ivan and Jesse showed the guests to their seats.

Bethany glanced at her soon-to-be husband. He looked very handsome in his black suit and black string tie. He smiled back at her. "It's not too late to call it off."

She shook her head. "I think it was too late the day I met you."

He snapped his fingers. "That's who we forgot to invite."

"Who?"

"Clarabelle."

Gemma entered with her parents. "A blessed Christmas to you and may you have a blessed life together."

"Thank you for agreeing to be my sidesitter," Bethany said.

"I am honored to be your attendant at your wedding. Michael, who is going to stand up with you?"

"Jesse has agreed to do me the favor."

Gemma made a sour face. "That man is as dense as a post." She went in to take her place on the front bench where Bethany would sit during the ceremony.

"What does she have against Jesse?" Michael asked.

"Nothing, except he hasn't noticed her in all the time she has been trying to catch his attention."

"She likes Jesse? Are you sure?"

"Very sure. Do you think this is everyone?" She glanced into the full living room, where the church benches had been set out in two rows for the men and the women.

"I think so."

"Where are the children?" Bethany looked around. "I hope Jenny is not getting her new dress dirty."

"I think she's trying to figure out some way to smuggle Sadie Sue in."

"As much as I like your dog, I'm not going to have her at my wedding."

He laughed and pointed up the stairwell. "I wouldn't be too sure about that."

Jenny was kneeling at the top of the steps with Sadie Sue lying beside her. The two of them scurried back down the hall when they realized they had been spotted.

"Do you want me to speak to her?" he asked.

"*Nee*, she knows better. She will behave. I hope."

The bishop came up to them. "Are you ready?"

They smiled at each other and nodded. "We're ready," they said in unison.

While the preparations had been rushed, the ceremony itself went off without a hitch. The bishop was short-winded for a change and the preaching lasted only three hours. As Bethany stood beside Michael in front of the bishop, she couldn't help but realize how very blessed she was to have found the perfect man. She couldn't stop smiling.

Afterward, Bethany went upstairs to change her black *kapp* for a white one. In the corner of the room facing the front door, the Eck, or the "corner table," was quickly set up for the wedding party.

When it was ready, Michael took his place with Jesse and Ivan seated to his right. Bethany was ushered back in and took her seat at his left-hand side. It symbolized the place she would occupy in his buggy and in his life. Her cheeks were rosy red and her eyes sparkled with happiness. They clasped hands underneath the table. Michael squeezed her fingers. "You are everything I could have asked for and so much more."

"I promise to try and be a *goot* wife to you," she said with a meekness he distrusted.

"Just be yourself. That will be good enough."

"You realize you get to choose the seating arrangements for the single people this evening, don't you?" Gemma asked.

Michael shrugged. "I haven't given it much thought."

"This might be the first wedding in New Covenant but I'm going to make sure it isn't the last," Bethany said with a wink at her friend.

Jenny sat on the other side of Gemma. "Are you going to pick a husband for me?"

"I may just do that." She smiled at her sister.

Michael leaned back in his seat. "Are you taking up matchmaking now?"

She chuckled. "Clarabelle is my only local competition. I think I can do better than her."

He leaned close to her. "The old cow did right by me."

"I beg to differ. She never once mentioned your name."

"Do you know what?"

"What?" she asked, intrigued by the light in his eyes.

"I can't wait to kiss you again."

Bethany felt the heat rush to her face. "I can't wait for that myself, my husband."

* * * * *

If you enjoyed this story,
look for these other Amish stories
by Patricia Davids:

An Amish Harvest
An Amish Noel
His Amish Teacher
Their Pretend Amish Courtship
Amish Christmas Twins
An Unexpected Amish Romance
His New Amish Family

Dear Reader,

This is the first book in my new Amish series set in Maine. I hope you have enjoyed the story. In case you haven't noticed, I am a dog lover. The remarkable Sadie Sue was patterned after my own dog Sadie. Sadly she is no longer with us but we have wonderful memories of her happy personality and relentless drive to fetch the ball, fetch the ball.

PTSD is a disorder that has been in the news a lot in recent years. Many of our soldiers are returning to civilian life crippled by this devastating disorder. More research is needed to combat this problem but therapy dogs have been shown to have a positive effect on the men and women who own them. I have limited knowledge of the disorder and this is not meant to be a tutorial on the subject. Any mistakes or incorrect assumptions are purely my own.

Blessings to all,
Patricia Davids

Get 4 FREE REWARDS!

We'll send you 2 FREE Books plus 2 FREE Mystery Gifts.

Love Inspired® Suspense books feature Christian characters facing challenges to their faith... and lives.

FREE
Value Over
$20

HOME on the RANCH

YES! Please send me the **Home on the Ranch Collection** in Larger Print. This collection begins with 3 FREE books and 2 FREE gifts in the first shipment. Along with my 3 free books, I'll also get the next 4 books from the Home on the Ranch Collection, in LARGER PRINT, which I may either return and owe nothing, or keep for the low price of $5.24 U.S./ $5.89 CDN each plus $2.99 for shipping and handling per shipment*. If I decide to continue, about once a month for 8 months I will get 6 or 7 more books, but will only need to pay for 4. That means 2 or 3 books in every shipment will be FREE! If I decide to keep the entire collection, I'll have paid for only 32 books because 19 books are FREE! I understand that accepting the 3 free books and gifts places me under no obligation to buy anything. I can always return a shipment and cancel at any time. My free books and gifts are mine to keep no matter what I decide.

268 HCN 3760 468 HCN 3760

Name   (PLEASE PRINT)

Address   Apt. #

City   State/Prov.   Zip/Postal Code

Signature (if under 18, a parent or guardian must sign)

Mail to the **Reader Service:**

IN U.S.A.: P.O. Box 1341, Buffalo, New York 14240-8531
IN CANADA: P.O. Box 603, Fort Erie, Ontario L2A 5X3

* Terms and prices subject to change without notice. Prices do not include applicable taxes. Sales tax applicable in NY. Canadian residents will be charged applicable taxes. This offer is limited to one order per household. All orders subject to approval. Credit or debit balances in a customer's account(s) may be offset by any other outstanding balance owed by or to the customer. Please allow 3 to 4 weeks for delivery. Offer available while quantities last. Offer not available to Quebec residents.

HRCBPA18R

READERSERVICE.COM

Manage your account online!

- Review your order history
- Manage your payments
- Update your address

> **We've designed the Reader Service website just for you.**

Enjoy all the features!

- Discover new series available to you, and read excerpts from any series.
- Respond to mailings and special monthly offers.
- Browse the Bonus Bucks catalog and online-only exculsives.
- Share your feedback.

Visit us at:

ReaderService.com

RS16R